The Name Game

Muncy G. Chapman

ISBN 1-59310-739-0

Cover image illustration by Jocelyne Bouchard.

Published by Humble Creek, P.O. Box 719, Uhrichsville, Ohio 44683

Printed in the United States of America.
5 4 3 2 1

MUNCY G. CHAPMAN

Muncy lives in Florida with her husband of over fifty years. With four happily married children and eleven grandchildren all living within the state, she finds plenty to keep her busy. She and her husband collaborated to write a Florida historical novel, "Wiregrass Country," which was published in 1998. She has won awards for her poetry, short stories, and newspaper articles. Muncy also likes to sew, cook, play the piano, and of course write! She takes an active roll in her church, especially in its ministries to shut-ins and children. Muncy sees her writing as a Christian ministry and is thankful God has given her the desire and resources to pursue this exciting challenge.

Lovingly dedicated to the remarkable ladies
of the Christine Evans Circle in Wauchula, Florida

Prologue

"I predict that you'll be coming back to New York within six months," Hal warned her. "And when you do, I'll still be here waiting for you."

Meg shook her head, and her heavy chestnut hair swirled and settled around her slim shoulders. "You still don't understand, do you, Hal?"

"No, I guess I'll have to admit that I don't. Want to tell me again why you're willing to leave an on-campus luxury apartment and a job as guidance counselor at the most prestigious girls' school in New York to take up residence in some isolated mountain community in North Carolina?"

"I'm certainly willing to agree that Hidden Oaks is a top-rated school, Hal, and you as headmaster must feel a great deal of personal satisfaction in its success. But I'm terribly excited about this move I'm about to make, and I wish you would try to share a little of my elation. Of course, teaching at Mountain View Community School is going to take some major adjusting on my part, but it sounds like a real challenge."

"I can't imagine your returning to the classroom, and a multilevel grade at that. Your training and expertise as a guidance counselor will be wasted on those rural mountain kids."

"I don't think so. At least, I hope not. Just because I won't have a nameplate hanging over my door with that designation doesn't mean I can't continue to guide and counsel my students."

"Have you stopped to consider that your paycheck will be exactly one-quarter the size of your present one?"

Meg ran her fingers through her hair and sighed. "We've been over all of this before, Hal. I've already made up my mind. I'm not going to try to justify my decision, and you have no right to question it."

"Then where does that leave me, Meg? What about us?"

Meg gentled her voice and tried to soften the impact of her words. "There is no us, Hal, and there never has been. I've never encouraged you to believe otherwise. I've given you no commitment, and I've asked none of you. I do care deeply for you—I truly do—but I'm not in the market for romance with you or anyone else right now, not until I've had a chance to satisfy at least some of my personal goals." She reached across the table to touch his hand. "You are a wonderful friend, one of the best I've ever had, and I'll always treasure what we've been to each other."

Meg's eyes misted, remembering how Hal had stood by her these last few months through the death of her last living relative, her beloved grandmother, and the painful weeks that followed. In truth, she did love this kind and gentle man, but not in the romantic sense that he kept pressing for.

Meg had received the sad and unexpected news of Gran's death in the middle of the last semester of the school year. The hasty round trip to North Carolina for the funeral, the meeting with lawyers, the swarms of friends who had tried to bring comfort—those things all swirled together in her memory in one sorrowful blur.

In the final days of the school year, Meg had tried hard not to let her own personal grief overshadow the relatively trivial problems of the teenage girls she was hired to counsel. Through her faith in God, she found the strength to move from one day to the next. And there were two other things that had helped to sustain her: the steadfast support of her friend, Hal Garrison, and her firm resolution that when school was over, she would return to Gran's North Carolina chalet. There she would find her peace in the shadow of the hills that she would eventually learn to call home.

To Meg, this seemed a logical decision. Throughout her childhood, midst the trauma of bickering parents who seldom took time to acknowledge her existence, she had always thought of Gran's house as her respite from the storms of life, and Gran had always been there for her, waiting with open arms and with no questions asked.

Meg's stormy home life was at least partially responsible for her decision to major in child guidance when she went away to college. She felt strongly that no child should have to live with the mistrust and rejection, the deceit and broken promises that had plagued her during her formative years. Perhaps the lingering scars of those years were the reason that she now felt no compelling urgency to marry and have a home of her own. Although she did not completely buy into her mother's theory that "all men are liars who can never be trusted," she decided early on that if and when she ever did marry, she would be careful to choose a lifetime partner who was open and honest and completely trustworthy.

Each year, as a child, Meg had looked forward to summer days that she could spend roaming the North Carolina foothills, wading in the cold, rocky creeks, picking berries, and standing beside Gran in the kitchen, watching her turn out pies and biscuits and jams along with generous portions of unconditional love and understanding. Gran had been her best friend, someone she could talk to about anything without fear of judgment or recrimination.

Together they had attended the small country church with the high wooden steeple, where an old iron bell echoed through the mountains and called them to worship each Sunday morning.

It was in that very church, when she was twelve years old, that Meg had given her heart to the Lord and discovered a joy beyond any she had ever imagined. She had been perplexed by Gran's tears that day and had not understood until many years later that tears can spring from happiness as easily as from grief.

Meg had a deep yearning to return to that tranquil place where she had experienced so much love and happiness. There her spirit would be renewed, her faith would be rekindled, and she would find peace for her troubled heart.

And there was another yearning in her heart that was harder to define. Because of her grandmother's guidance and example, Meg's life had been heaped with blessings, and now she wanted to give something back to a world that had given her so much.

She had tried to explain this to Hal one evening as they walked home together after a concert, but he had stared at her as though she were speaking in a foreign language. "You're selling yourself short," he argued. "Just look at the work you are doing here at this school. You give a big part of yourself to these girls every day of your life, and they all love you for it."

"I know they do, and I love them, too, but I want to go where I'm really needed, Hal."

"You're needed right here, Meg. If you don't believe me, just ask a dozen of our students and see what they tell you."

"Of course they'll say they need me," Meg agreed. "They'll also tell you that they need designer jeans, a date for the prom, and Cliff Notes so that they won't have to read a book they don't have time for."

She could hardly blame Hal for his lack of understanding, because she was not sure that she totally understood all of these things herself.

But Hal finally accepted her decision because he had no other choice. "I'll call you often, Meg. Don't let pride get in your way if you wake up one morning and realize that you've made a mistake. As long as I have any say in the matter, there will always be a place for you here at Hidden Oaks. Don't be too stubborn to come home."

Chapter 1

Meg sat at her kitchen table and graded the last exam. Recording the scores in her black leather book, she beamed a satisfied smile. The final grade of each of her twenty-seven students had risen several points since she had taken over their classroom last September, putting to rest her fears that teaching four levels in the same room would prove an impossible task.

Mountain View Community School, an unpretentious, rectangular building, consisted of two large, unconnected rooms with entrances located on opposite sides of the wooden structure. Perched on the mountainside, it sat in isolation amid tall, stately pines and poplar trees, drawing children from all four sides of the neighboring woods. Meg's class was made up of fifth- through eighth-grade students, while Claire Ellison taught the younger children in the other classroom. After students completed eighth grade, they were bused into the consolidated high school located in nearby Shady Valley.

Not only was the primitive environment of Mountain View Community School different from the impressive New York boarding school Meg had left behind exactly a year ago, but the students themselves were an entirely different breed. Unconcerned about the brand names of their shoes and clothes, these boys and girls seemed to realize that education was both a privilege and a responsibility, and they drank up the knowledge she served them like camels at an oasis. And for the first time in her life, Meg felt really *needed*.

On the whole, Meg considered her first year in Mountain View a success story. Others would disagree, of course, depending upon how they measured success. But her yardstick was placed on the minds and hearts of her students and on her own personal growth, and those things were sometimes hard to measure.

Only one student had caused her to question her decision about coming to the rural classroom: Billy McLendon. A wiry, likeable youngster whose rusty hair matched the color of his numerous freckles, Billy himself was not the problem; the problem was Billy's father.

Bud McLendon had stormed into her classroom the first week of school, smelling strongly of whiskey and rancid sweat, hurling threats at her across the room full of astonished and terrified children. "Are you the new teacher from the city that's been readin' the Bible to these younguns?" He pushed his bulky frame through the doorway and staggered toward the front of the class where Meg stood writing the day's history assignment on the blackboard.

Billy McLendon jumped up from his desk and ran to his father's side, tugging on his burly arm. "Daddy, *please!*"

"Git out of my way." The drunken man shoved his son so roughly that the tormented youth fell against one of the desks, and books and papers flew everywhere.

Meg was frightened out of her wits, but she knew better than to reveal her fears to the brawny bully she faced. Instead, she took a step toward him. "Mr. McLendon, I would like to discuss this matter with you in private. Could you come back at three o'clock after the children have been dismissed? I'll be glad to show you all the resource materials I use in this class, and we can go over your grievances."

"Listen here, lady, I got nothin' to discuss with you. You just better hear what I'm tellin' you." He pointed his finger in her face to emphasize his words. "We got laws about such as you, and I know my rights. If I hear tell of you teachin' my youngun from the Bible, you'll hear from me in a way you won't like. They's people around these parts that's tried to cross Bud McLendon before, and some of them didn't live long enough to regret it." He turned and staggered out the door, almost falling over the threshold.

Meg tried to keep her hands from shaking as she righted the overturned desk and put the books and papers back into place. She picked up her history textbook and proceeded with the lesson. The students were unusually quiet and attentive for the remainder of the day, except for Billy, who buried his head in his arms on his desktop. Meg's heart went out to the boy, but to save him further embarrassment, she ignored him.

That was the first of several episodes. She reported each incident to the county school superintendent who made sporadic visits to the little school, and eventually the law had stepped in. Bud McLendon had spent ten days in the local jail, and upon his release, he had been prohibited from putting his feet on school property.

For the rest of the school year, Billy's attendance was spasmodic, and he often appeared with unexplained bruises on his body. He became more and more withdrawn. Then midway through the term, he had transferred to another school district, and Meg was relieved to hear that Billy had been taken from his home and placed in the care of foster parents.

"What about his mother?" Meg asked Claire one afternoon after all the children had been dismissed.

"All I know is hearsay," Claire admitted. "Rumor is that she got fed up with Bud's abuse, and one day she ran off with an itinerant farm-supply salesman. Poor little Billy was just a toddler then, left to fend for himself. He was in my classroom last year, and I love that child, but his father has created problems for us before. You'd better be careful in your dealings with him. He's very mean and sneaky."

But not all of Meg's experiences at Mountain View Community School had been unpleasant. On the plus side, the test scores she recorded in her book today gave evidence as to just how far most of her students had advanced academically.

In addition to teaching the basic educational material, Meg tried to build character and integrity in her pupils. Her training in counseling had enabled her to help several boys and girls whose progress was impeded by a lack of self-esteem. Thus, she was able to deny Hal's prediction that her training would be wasted here.

And yes, she did use the Bible in her classroom. Most of her students came from fundamental Christian homes and attended church services regularly, and she had been instrumental in persuading several others to enroll in Sunday school. By her measurements, she could declare emphatically that the past year had been an extremely rewarding one.

Meg closed her grade book and eyed the stack of unopened mail that she had dropped on her table when she got home from school this afternoon. She decided to make a pot of coffee before she began the depressing job of looking at her bills. Each month she faced the same struggle of trying to keep her checks within the range of the small deposit of her teacher's salary. As long as there were no extras, she could just about break even. But the "extras" were slowly eroding the meager savings she had deposited when she took up residence here in the house Gran had left to her.

She had assumed that not having to pay rent would allow her to add regularly to her savings account instead of depleting it, but she had forgotten to consider things like property taxes and homeowner's insurance and maintenance costs, things that had never been hers to worry about before.

She flipped through her mail, deliberately ignoring the envelopes with cellophane windows. The bills could wait until later, after she had enjoyed her coffee. There was a card from the church reminding her of the cake that she had pledged for Saturday's bake sale, and there was a letter from Hal. After supper, she would look through her recipe file for Gran's apple cake recipe, and she would read Hal's letter for "dessert." Right now, the rhythmic pulsation of her coffeepot and its tempting aroma sent a message she could not refuse.

She filled a ceramic mug with the fresh, steaming coffee and carried it through the living room onto her redwood deck. Although her kitchen and back porch were nearly level with her backyard, the slope of the mountain gave rise to her living room and the front deck that spanned the width of her house. This deck that seemed to be floating in space had always been her favorite spot in the whole world! She and Gran had spent countless hours relaxing in the wicker chairs or pushing the big porch swing back and forth with their toes as they looked out over the majestic mountains and talked. When Meg sat in the swing now, she could almost sense Gran's presence here beside her, stroking her hair and generously offering her words of wisdom.

Two squirrels joined Meg on the deck and made themselves at home, feasting on acorns that fell from the surrounding trees. A cardinal and a sparrow settled on opposite sides of a bird feeder that hung from the porch lintel, and a hummingbird hovered over a jar of sweet, red nectar that Meg had prepared for him earlier that morning.

Meg sipped the hot coffee and kicked off her shoes. Here midst the mountains, she could almost forget the worrisome bills that waited for her on the kitchen table. But sooner or later, she was going to have to face up to reality. She would receive her last check from the county next week, and after that, there would be no more income until fall. How could she make ends meet through the summer?

Last year, she had delved into her savings for moving expenses and for the things she needed to convert this house into her permanent home. She still had a little of that nest egg left, but if she began using her dwindling savings for living expenses, she would eventually have to admit defeat and leave this place she had grown to love so much. But that was an option she refused to even consider. There had to be some other way. She had been praying about it for weeks, and although God had not provided her with an answer yet, she felt that He had led her to this place for a purpose, and she had unwavering faith that He would see her through.

From twelve feet below, she could hear the rush of water over rocks in the winding brook that defined her property line. This was her home now, and she loved every inch of it.

As shards of afternoon sun filtered through the surrounding trees, reflecting their lacy pattern across her porch, she prayed, *Lord, You have called me to this peaceful place, and given me meaningful work to do here. I don't want to let You down, but I just don't know how to make it the rest of the way on my own. Please lead me and show me what to do.*

The familiar warmth of answered prayer swept through her. *Lo, I am with you always!* Meg did not know what her answers would be, but she was very sure where they would come from.

Chapter 2

Sitting at her kitchen table, Meg used a ballpoint pen to draw a vertical line down the length of her yellow legal pad, dividing the page into two even columns. She headed the column on the left side, "Expenses." Here she listed all of her regular expenses, and added a miscellaneous fund for the unexpected things that seemed to crop up with irritating regularity. On the other side of her page, she wrote "Income." That column was easy to fill out. She had only two sources of income to consider: her teacher's salary and the interest on her savings account, a pittance at best and growing even smaller as her bank balance decreased.

The trick was going to be in deciding how to diminish the figures on the left side of her page while expanding the figures in the right-hand column. She studied each expense item. Already she was a miser when it came to electricity, and while she considered her telephone a necessity as well as a convenience, she seldom made long-distance calls, so there was no fat she could trim from her budget in either of those items. Food? She had a vegetable garden, and she clipped coupons from her Sunday paper to pinch pennies when she shopped for groceries. She considered getting a cow or some chickens, but she abandoned that idea before it had a chance to grow roots. She had no idea how one coaxed milk from a cow, and she certainly would never be able to kill a chicken! That very thought was enough to make a vegetarian of her for life! How about her church donation? No, she had always tithed her salary, and she was not going to change that practice now. She would have to find some other expenditure to trim because she certainly wouldn't change that!

She dragged her pencil down the column of expenses and gave a weary sigh. She was sure the answer to her problems could not be found there.

On the other side of her paper, she studied the two entries. Teacher's salary. She had been promised a small raise in September, but September was three months away. Besides, in this rural area, the amount of her increase would not likely be great enough to affect her lifestyle. Interest income? As she bit into her savings to cover expenses, her interest income was moving in the wrong direction. The answer seemed simple enough:

She *must* find an additional source of income.

Three whole months stretched in front of her; months she had counted on using to paint the house, work in her garden, sew clothes for the coming school year, put up summer jams and jellies, and maybe just possibly indulge herself with a few days of doing absolutely nothing. Could she find some kind of job that would bring in a little extra income and still allow her time to do all the chores she was saving for summer?

The telephone interrupted her thoughts, and she pushed herself up from her chair to answer it. "Hello?"

"Hi, Meg! It's me, Sandy. Am I interrupting anything?"

"I'll say, and a mighty pleasant interruption it is! I'm working on my budget."

Meg heard a mock groan and then laughter on the other end of the line. Sandy could afford to laugh. She had a good job as a salesperson in a local real estate office and a husband who worked for the power company. Her children were grown, and Sandy was learning to cope with an empty nest. "What's happening over your way, Sandy?"

"Over her way" was about half a mile down the curving mountain road, and the two women, in spite of a twenty-year age difference, had become good friends during the past year, since Meg had become a resident of the Mountain View community.

"I just made a blackberry cobbler, and the coffee's hot. Jim's gone to a meeting, and I'm home alone. Why don't you take a break from your budget and come down for a while?"

"Mm! You know how to tweak my vulnerable spots, don't you? But really, Sandy, if I come down, I can't stay long. I have to make something for the Saturday bake sale, and my laundry is backed up, and there's still a lot to do for the one remaining week of school."

❧

"This is wonderful, Sandy," Meg declared, scraping up the last bite of cobbler from her plate. "How do you find time to pick blackberries, bake, and keep up with all your housework while holding down a full-time job?"

"I picked these berries after supper last night. Now that the days are getting longer, I love getting out after the sun goes down. But you're right, I have been busy lately. Our office has been a zoo! When school is out, I think half the population of Florida and Georgia want to bring their kids to the mountains for the summer, and I have to try to find them places to stay!"

"Is that a problem?"

"You'd better believe it! And you would never believe the seasonal rental prices! It almost makes me want to go somewhere else so that I could rent my own house out for a few weeks."

Meg turned that idea over in her mind. "Well, I could sure use the extra income myself, but the only problem is that I'd have nowhere else to go!"

Sandy laughed. "That's what it always comes down to with me, too, but it's fun to dream. I could do a lot with all that extra money."

"Speaking of extra money, you don't know of anyone willing to hire a lady of limited talents on a temporary basis this summer, do you?"

"You?"

"None other. I'd like to find some way to bring in a little extra money for the three months I'm out of school. I could qualify as a counselor at a summer camp, but those jobs usually pay almost nothing. In fact, they are often filled by volunteer workers. Let's face it; there's not much call for a teacher in the summertime, and I don't know how to do anything else."

"Can you type?"

"Yes, but I'm a little rusty."

"Listen, Meg, if you're really serious about this, you might be just the person my boss is looking for. Our receptionist just left to have a baby, and the rest of us have been taking turns filling in for her at the front desk, but now with the onslaught of summer people, we're snowed under. Patty wants to come back to work in the fall, so Mr. Hanson is trying to hold the job open for her. He's been interviewing students, trying to find one who might fill in just during the summer months, but so far, he hasn't found anyone he feels is mature enough to handle our clients. Why don't you come in after school tomorrow and talk to him?"

"Oh, Sandy. Do you really think he might hire me? I don't have any real estate experience."

"Neither did Patty. He just needs someone who is dependable and can meet the public, and you certainly meet both of those requirements. I'll make the appointment for you, and I'll even put in a good word for you in advance."

"You're terrific! And thanks for the cobbler and coffee, but honestly, I do have to run."

ෂ

Back in her own kitchen, Meg began to plan as she laid out the ingredients for her cake. Even if the pay turned out to be only minimum wage, working for three months in the real estate office would certainly take the edge off her immediate financial problems.

She sifted and measured the cake flour into a large mixing bowl, but she continued to plan ahead. She could not quit thinking about what

Sandy had said about summer renters. If Meg could think of some way to let out her house for the summer—but at this point, she drew a blank. She had nowhere else to go.

Meg scraped the batter into two round cake tins and put them in the preheated oven. While her cake was baking, Meg rounded up her dirty clothes and linens and piled them into a big plastic basket. Carrying her laundry, she crossed the back porch and headed down the steep incline that led to her basement. She had to step carefully to avoid slipping on the flat stones that had been strategically placed to form a descending walkway from the west side of her back porch, all the way down to the brook below.

Taking advantage of the mountain drop, Meg's basement was nestled neatly beneath the front half of her house and added a generous storage area as well as a laundry room.

She would have time to get her washing machine started before the cake was ready to come out of the oven. Then while the cake cooled, she could run back down to the lower level and put her clothes in the dryer.

How thankful she was that Gran had purchased a nearly new washing machine and dryer just a few months before her death. Meg arranged her clothes in the machine and added liquid detergent. She set the dial and heard the motor give a satisfying hum as it began its rhythmic churn.

An old sofa bed was shoved against the concrete block wall, and Meg sank down on it to catch her breath. The basement, which ran the expanse of her living room, front bedroom, and deck, was exactly half as big as her house upstairs. It was here that the idea struck her like a blackboard eraser aimed at her head. Her basement! It was fully wired with electricity, and there was even a metal shower stall and a toilet. With a small investment, she could turn this place into temporary quarters for the summer and find a renter for her upstairs! The idea excited her so that she almost forgot about the cake rising in the oven.

She raced outside and climbed the stepping stones, letting the basement screen door slam behind her. Why hadn't she thought of this idea before? The solution seemed so obvious, and so perfect for her needs.

As she removed her cake layers from the oven and positioned them on a rack to cool, she began to feel the first hint of misgivings. In the excitement of the moment, she had not paused to consider how she would feel about having someone else move into her home, eat meals from Gran's china, and move about among her personal belongings. She was not at all sure she could handle that. No, she would have to think of some other way to solve her problem.

If she was hired to work in the real estate office immediately after school ended, and if the pay was better than she had any right to expect, then maybe. . . She would go over her budget again tomorrow after her meeting with the real estate broker. With new figures to add to the income column, she would somehow find a way to balance the two.

Austin Bruce yanked the paper from his printer, wadded it in a tight ball, and threw it in the wastebasket to join the dozens of others just like it. He had read and heard about writer's block, but never before had he fallen victim to the malady himself.

For weeks, his historical novel had flowed along at a swift, smooth pace, and now that he was so close to the end of it, his mind was drawing a total blank. He kept returning to the first few chapters where he had been unable to satisfy himself with an adequate description of his protagonist. Perhaps because he could not draw a clear picture of her in his own mind, he was unable to convey a convincing description to his text. It didn't help that his editor had already called him twice this week, wanting to know when the final chapters would be ready. "Just give me a ball park figure, Austin. We have a publishing schedule to consider up here. Two weeks? Two months? Just tell me something."

How could he give her an answer that he did not have? Pushed for a reply, he had blurted out, "You'll have the complete manuscript by the end of summer. That's the best I can promise, Ramona."

He pushed himself away from his computer and paced the floor of his study. He looked out a multipaned bay window across the carefully manicured lawn of his north Florida home and tried to draw inspiration from his elegant surroundings. Maybe that was his trouble. Maybe he needed a change of scenery to stimulate his creativity. He had been holed up here in his study for weeks, with scarcely a break except for meals. If he could just get away for a few weeks. . . Yes, that was the answer. He'd call his travel agent first thing in the morning. Maybe he'd rent a cottage at the seashore, or perhaps in the mountains. Anywhere new and secluded would bring a refreshing change. His stagnant mental juices began to flow just thinking about it.

The good news and the bad news, Meg thought cynically as she turned her car toward home. The good news was that Mr. Hanson had hired her on the spot. She had agreed to begin work on the Monday after school ended. The bad news was that she would begin at the absolute bottom of the pay scale and would not be employed long enough to hope for anything more. Still, with careful planning, she would manage to get through the summer, and she would not have to let some stranger take over her home and its furnishings. It appalled her now in the light of day that she had even considered such an unpleasant idea.

She rounded the S-curve of the highway and slowed to turn off onto the unpaved road that wound up the mountainside to her house. She was just passing Sandy's house when her car gave a grinding gurgle, choked a few times, and then abruptly stopped. Steam rose in great clouds from beneath the hood, and the smell of burnt rubber permeated the surrounding air.

Meg stepped cautiously from her car and stood looking down at its hood. She stared helplessly at the menacing fog that enveloped the front of her car. She did not dare to raise the hood, and even if she did, the strange things that lurked beneath the hoods of cars were always a complete mystery to her. She would have to telephone the garage for a mechanic.

Frustration seized her when she looked around and realized that neither Sandy nor Jim would be home from work at this time of day, and there was no way she could get into their house to use their telephone. The nearest phone would be at her own house. Meg locked her car and began her half-mile hike up the mountain road toward home. Although walking was her favorite form of exercise, her high heels threw her precariously off balance as she limped up the road, and the rocky terrain made the thin soles of her shoes feel as though they were made of tissue paper.

Her poor feet! When she finally reached her back porch, the first thing that she did was shed her shoes. Then, unlocking her back door, in her stocking feet she stepped over the threshold, anticipating the feel of the smooth, cool vinyl of her kitchen floor. But immediately her relief turned to horror. In her absence, her kitchen floor had been transformed into a shallow lake.

Meg didn't shriek or scream; that was not her style. She simply threw up her hands and gaped in alarm. "What in the world has happened here?"

For a moment, she thought that she was going to be physically ill, but there was no time for that. She couldn't afford to indulge in self-pity when there was so much work staring her in the face.

First things first. She retrieved a string mop from its hook on the back porch and waded straight into the middle of the mess. Water splashed around her ankles, and her nylons felt like soggy gloves clinging to her feet.

She used her mop to soak up the water, squeezing it into a galvanized bucket. It took half an hour to dry the floor, empty her bucket, and determine the source of her trouble. The latter was the easiest part. Clearly, the water was coming from her refrigerator. She would have to call an electrician and hope that he would be able to come before any of her food spoiled.

She sank into the nearest chair, frustrated and exhausted. Mechanic bills! Electrician bills! Was there no end to her troubles? What if some other trouble popped up this summer! Where would she be?

Chapter 3

The final week of school gave Meg little time to think about her financial problems, but they lurked around the corner like a cunning fox waiting for his prey. In just seven days, this class of boys and girls would be only a memory, and Meg would be turning her attention to another job. And unlike her present occupation, this new position would be one for which she had neither training nor experience.

As much as she looked forward to a change of pace, saying good-bye to her students filled Meg with a bittersweet sadness mingled with pride in their yearlong achievements.

Even the boys and girls, restless from long hours of classroom confinement, lingered over her desk each afternoon, savoring their last hours together before the three-month break. Meg knew that some of them would never return. Instead, they would put down their schoolbooks and trade them for farm tools. Even the girls, once they reached their teens, were often needed to work in the apple orchards and fields or to help with domestic chores at home.

Meg ached to help them, especially the ones who seemed so eager to learn. Last spring, she had approached the county director of library systems in an effort to extend the privilege of reading to the people, adults as well as children, who lived in the rural areas like Mountain View. She had presented her self-organized campaign to every local meeting that would allow her a spot on its program. As a result, the county commissioners had launched a public drive to purchase a bookmobile, and several of the civic organizations in Shady Valley had pledged their support. Meg was proud and happy to know that her dream would soon become a reality.

On the last day of school, Meg's big desk was cluttered with gifts: a jar of watermelon-rind pickles, an embroidered tea towel made from a bleached flour sack, a loaf of fresh, homemade bread, a wise-looking owl skillfully carved from pecan wood. One after another, the children stepped forward to place their offerings on her desk. She heard words such as "Mama made this for you" and "My dad carved this hisself" and even "My parents told me to tell you 'thank you.'" Realizing the sacrificial nature of these gifts, Meg was both touched and embarrassed.

The entire day was given over to fun and games, and just before she dismissed the children, Meg gave each one a book to keep. For many, these would be the only books they owned. Having the regular services of a bookmobile in this area would truly be a godsend for these boys and girls.

She stood in the doorway of the schoolhouse and watched them leave, running, skipping, yelling, relishing their new freedom. Many of them turned back to wave to her.

In the classroom next door, Claire had dismissed the younger children earlier and left to go home, leaving Meg alone in the old wooden structure where she had taught for the past nine months. She washed the blackboard and put the pieces of chalk in a tin box on the shelf.

There was talk of closing this rural two-room school and busing the area children to one of the consolidated schools in Shady Valley. Economically, Meg knew that this made sense for the county, but the extended hours would work a hardship on the farming families who depended on their children's after-school help, and the Mountain View parents vigorously protested all efforts to change the *status quo*.

Meg walked among the empty desks, fondly remembering each child. She thought of Lucy-Ann, the twelve-year-old girl who in previous years had been placed in a group of slow learners simply because she was too shy to participate. Meg's counseling skills had drawn Lucy-Ann out of her shell and revealed that, contrary to the results reported in earlier diagnostic testing, she was an unusually bright child. And of course, there was Billy McLendon, whose big, sad eyes concealed secrets too dark to fathom. Meg wondered if he was happy in his new home. At least she knew that he would be safe!

She had a special empathy for children like Billy, for although she had never suffered physical abuse, she still carried the scars of psychological abuse meted out by her parents, who would have quickly denied any such accusations. In fact, they had probably deceived themselves into believing that they were providing a good home for their daughter. *Deceit*—what an ugly word!

As she passed the empty desks, Meg's mind played back over the school year, and she offered an individual prayer for each child, thanking God for giving her the tools to help them. She had grown to love them all, even the least lovable ones, the few who seemed to take great delight in trying her patience. Thoughts of them brought a smile to her lips. They had become her children, her family, and she would miss them now that summer was here.

Meg gathered her collection of gifts and put these treasured items in her canvas tote, smiling as she ran her fingers over their surfaces. At the end of school last year in New York, her students had gifted her with expensive perfumes, silk scarves, and costume jewelry, purchased with plastic credit cards and little emotion. But because these handmade gifts she received today were born of love and personal sacrifice, she valued them all the more.

At Hidden Oaks School for Girls in New York, hundreds of girls would now be packing to go home for the summer. Meg had loved those girls, too; they were good girls, for the most part. She hoped that they would gain the wisdom and maturity to eat well from the silver spoons thrust into their mouths since birth. If they made good choices, life could be a good deal easier for them than for the children here at Mountain View.

Hal would be leaving New York today, too, for an extended Mediterranean cruise. He had pleaded with Meg to go with him. As headmaster of Hidden Oaks, with an on-campus apartment, his living expenses were small and his salary generous. He could well afford luxurious vacations each summer.

"Marry me, Meg, and then we'll make this cruise our honeymoon."

If Meg had said yes, she would now be preparing to embark on an adventurous journey instead of a new job for which she felt ill prepared.

Hal had told her she was making a mistake. If she was not yet ready for marriage, then they could book separate passages on the cruise, he suggested, and use this summer to strengthen and define their feelings for each other. Had her decision to leave a secure job and a man who cared for her been a mistake? Was it possible that Hal might be right? But Meg dismissed that idea as quickly as it had popped into her head.

Her whole purpose in coming to Mountain View was to make a meaningful contribution of her talents, and she felt a warm glow of satisfaction in her accomplishments of the past months. She had no reason to feel that the next school year would be any different.

As to what the next three months would bring, Meg would not dare to venture a guess. Although the new job did not sound difficult, it was totally out of her area of expertise. During her interview with Mr. Hanson, she had been so determined to make a good impression that she had scarcely thought to ask him just what he would expect of her. Would he be disappointed to learn that she was only a mediocre typist and lacked basic office skills? Sandy had only mentioned answering the phone. Surely she could handle that, but she had a sneaky suspicion that the job might involve more. Then again, at the salary Mr. Hanson had quoted, he could not have been expecting an office paragon. She would give Mr. Hanson her best efforts and hope that they would be enough. And in turn, she would use her salary to bail herself out of her present problems and hope that *it* would be enough.

Meg had just one short weekend to call her own, to do all the things she had saved for the entire summer. In just three short days, Meg Donnelly, schoolteacher, would turn into Meg Donnelly, office receptionist. There was no time to waste.

She finished cleaning out her desk, dusted the blackboard erasers, and restored order to the schoolroom. Then she picked up her purse and headed for the door. It was time to go home.

Chapter 4

On Monday morning, Meg sat at an unfamiliar desk, smaller than the one in her classroom, and infinitely less cluttered. A telephone, a hand-painted jar filled with an assortment of pens and pencils, a stenographer's pad, and a vase containing a single red rose were displayed in an orderly arrangement on a surface so shiny that Meg could see a reflection of her face staring back at herself.

The telephone had a musical tinkle. "Hanson Realty," she answered. "How may I direct your call?" Before she could press a button to make the proper connection, her phone was ringing again. And so it had been all through the hectic morning. When the phone wasn't ringing, customers were filing through the front door, and it was Meg's job to welcome them and make them feel at home until one of the licensed agents could meet with them. Meg could certainly understand the firm's need of someone to fill this position, because although her work had been as simple as child's play, it required almost constant attention. Her job seemed relatively unimportant, but at least she was able to free up time for the people who did the real work around here.

"How's it going, Miss Donnelly?" A deep voice drew Meg's attention to the tall, lean man who stood beside her desk. His thick gray hair added a touch of distinction to his appearance. "How are you bearing up under the pressure?"

"Oh, Mr. Hanson!" She returned his friendly smile. "I'm getting along just fine—at least I think I am. You don't know what pressure is until you've tried to control a classroom of children whose ages range from ten to fifteen! And this office is so well organized that my contribution here seems almost insignificant."

"Well, let me assure you that what you are doing here is far from insignificant! Our entire staff of agents stands to benefit from your presence this summer, Miss Donnelly. We all hope that you find your work here pleasant, and if ever there is anything that we can do to help you, I hope that you will ask."

"Thank you, Mr. Hanson. I'm glad for the chance to work here, and I'll do my best to make the rest of you glad as well."

Mr. Hanson raised his left arm and looked at his watch. "It's almost noon. If you'd like to break for lunch now, go ahead. I'll find someone to cover your desk for an hour. We're usually not too busy during the middle part of the day anyway."

"Thanks," Meg said, reaching into the desk drawer for her purse. "I'll wash my hands and then run down to the corner café for a sandwich. I won't be out long."

On her way to the rest room, she met Sandy in the hall. Meg was accustomed to seeing Sandy in a pair of faded blue jeans and an old T-shirt, but today her neighbor looked chic and professional in a tailored coral suit and matching high heels as she greeted Meg with a big smile. "How are you holding up on your first day? I hear you're doing just great!"

"Oh, Sandy, I hope so. All I've done is answer the phone and direct calls and play hostess to the walk-ins, but it's been interesting. I'm on my way to wash up for a lunch break. Can you join me?"

"Sure. Give me ten minutes to log off of my computer, and I'll meet you. Where do you want to go?"

In her determination to hold down her living expenses, Meg had thought of bringing a simple peanut butter sandwich from home this morning, but on her first day, she had decided that it might be better to wait to see what others did. She desperately wanted to make a good impression, and she certainly did not want to appear cheap. "I thought I'd grab a bowl of soup at that little café on the corner. I ate a big breakfast, so I'm not very hungry."

"Get a booth and save a place for me. Go ahead and order me a burger and fries, and I'll be along in a jiffy."

Sitting in the booth waiting for her friend, Meg scanned the menu. The prices seemed reasonable, so she ordered a bowl of homemade vegetable soup and a tossed salad, along with the order for Sandy.

Minutes later, Sandy slid into the space across from her just as the waitress delivered their plates to the table. "Looks like I got here at just the right time," she declared, settling herself on the red plastic upholstery. "I'm glad for a chance to chat. Did they deliver your new refrigerator yet?"

"Herman's Appliances delivered it yesterday. It's not exactly a *new* refrigerator, but at least it seems to be working, and they did give me a one-year guarantee."

"Did you trade in your old one?"

"No, they weren't able to offer me anything for it because it was so old, but they did move it into the basement for me, and replaced a hose so that it runs okay for now. The appliance repairman said I shouldn't count on its lasting very long. He warned me that the motor was pretty corroded and could go out at any time, but he said I might as well use it for extra cold storage space for as long as it lasts."

"You were smart to go ahead and replace it now. Another episode like the one you had last week, and your pretty kitchen floor could be ruined."

"It's lucky I came home when I did. Another hour and the water would have seeped into my living room carpet. I couldn't take a chance on that happening again. At least in the basement, there's not much that water would damage."

The café was filling rapidly with noontime workers. Sandy motioned to two women who were standing just inside the door waiting for a table. "Lucy, Gina, over here!" In an aside to Meg, she said, "You don't mind sharing our booth with them, do you? They work in the courthouse across the street."

"No, of course not."

"You'll like them," Sandy said, as the women approached.

As introductions were made, Meg realized that she would not have the opportunity to discuss privately with Sandy the thoughts that had been churning in her head all morning. Perhaps she would call her tonight.

ര

"Austin, I know just the place!" the travel agent's cheery voice assured him. "There's a gorgeous hotel nestled in the Smoky Mountains near Asheville that has everything you could possibly want. Scenery, entertainment, good food, luxury accommodations, a Jacuzzi in every room—"

"Hold it, Connie. I don't think you understand. I don't want a holiday; I want a getaway. Just something simple and secluded, away from the madding crowds, where I can work in uninterrupted silence."

"Well, yes, of course, but you'll still need to think about your meals and—"

"Trust me, Connie. I know how to boil an egg. What I need is food for my *soul*, not for my belly. Just find me the most secluded spot in the universe, and leave the rest of it to me."

"If you say so, Austin, but I think the charm of life as a country hermit will wear thin pretty fast for a man who's accustomed to being pampered by a first-rate staff of servants. Besides, my files don't include listings for caves, but if you insist, then I'll look around and see what I can come up with."

"Do that, Connie. With your knack for accomplishing the impossible, I'm sure you'll turn up just the cave I've been looking for. And just to show my appreciation, why don't I take you out for dinner tonight?"

"Only if you promise it won't be cooked on a stick over an open fire in the wilderness."

"You'll just have to take your chances. I'll pick you up at seven."

Meg parked her car by the back porch and entered her house through the kitchen. The almost-new refrigerator resonated a comforting hum, and the floor was as dry as the Sahara Desert. She might believe that things were beginning to turn around for her if it were not for the two new bills staring her in the face!

Three hundred dollars for the refrigerator and two hundred eighty-eight dollars for automobile repair! What was a carburetor, anyway? She had no idea, but at least her car was running again. Her first two weeks' salary was already spent before she even received it. She had the strange sensation of trying to run on a treadmill that was moving too fast, edging her backwards step by frantic step.

When the phone rang, she hoped that it would be Sandy. She needed to talk to her as soon as possible.

"Hello?"

"Hello, Meg. How's my favorite pioneer?"

She recognized the familiar voice and smiled. "Hal. How nice of you to call! Is this just a city slicker's weekly check on the life of a pioneer, or is something big going on that you called to share?"

"Both, actually. But mainly I wanted to let you know that the guidance counselor who replaced you here at the school is marrying and moving on. Your old position is up for grabs, and you know that you'd be given first priority if I told the board that you were coming back. And listen to this: The board has approved a six percent raise for the entire faculty. Now, is that good news or what?"

"That's wonderful, Hal. You and the others on staff deserve every penny of that raise, and I'm happy for you."

"You're ignoring the most important part, Meg. You know I haven't pushed you about this before. I understood your need to go back and revive your roots, to prove something to yourself. But you've done that now, and as your friend, I want to urge you to think about coming home."

"Hal, I *am* home."

"Okay, okay. A poor choice of words on my part. But, Meg, don't give me an answer today. Just promise me you'll think about the opportunities waiting for you here in New York. You have so many friends who would be happy to see you return to the school, and as far as career advancement, well, a chance like this doesn't happen every day!"

"Hal, you're sweet to think of me, and I really do appreciate it. You're still right at the top of my list of best friends."

"So will you think about it? That's all I'm asking."

"I'll think about it," she promised before saying good-bye.

She cradled her head in her hands and tried to settle her spinning thoughts. The school in New York had provided her with a good life and a stable income. Perhaps Hal was right. If she returned to New York, she might even be able to afford to keep her mountain home and come here for vacations in the summer months. Wasn't that better than having strangers move into her home among all her treasured memories?

But what about the children of the Mountain View neighborhood who depended on her? Who would step into her place? It was not easy to entice a good teacher to accept an appointment out here in the mountain wilderness. Could she in clear conscience turn her back on these children who needed her?

She needed an objective opinion. She dialed Sandy's number, and the sound of her friend's voice on the other end of the line brought her emotions to the surface so that she had to pause before she could speak.

"Meg, is that you? What's wrong? Is your kitchen flooded again?"

"No–no, it's nothing like that. I guess I just need a sounding board."

"Don't even try to tell me about it over the phone. I'll be at your house in ten minutes."

Sandy came into Meg's kitchen without knocking, carrying a covered casserole in her hands. "Do me a favor and finish this," she said, putting the warm dish on the counter. "I fixed this chicken and rice thing for supper last night, and Jim hates to be served leftovers."

Meg gave her a hug. "Oh, Sandy, you're such a good neighbor, and I'm sorry to be such a bother. I'm just feeling a bit overwhelmed, that's all. But I keep praying about it, and I know that in the end, everything will work out for the best."

"Let's go out on the deck right now and pray about it together," Sandy suggested, grabbing Meg's hand and leading her toward the living room door. "Whatever the problem is, God will help us get you through it, Meg."

Austin smiled at his silver-haired dinner companion across the candlelit dinner table. He and Connie had been close friends for over two years, ever since she had arranged an itinerary for his first book tour, and long before either of them dreamed that his novels would ever head the best-seller list. He often sought the wisdom of her sage advice.

"What's this sudden fetish about running away, Austin? I thought you had a new novel to finish."

"I do, Connie. In fact, Ramona is putting so much pressure on me to finish that I feel she is at least partially the cause of my mental stagnation."

"Ramona. . .she's your New York agent, isn't she?"

"Yes!" Austin spoke as though the thought pained him. "In all fairness, I must admit she's done a very good job for me in the past, but for some reason, I seem to be at a standstill. I'm reaching for something, but I can't even tell you what it is."

"Maybe running away is not the answer. I can't imagine that living a hermit's life will fill you with new ideas and inspiration."

"You're right, of course. The fact is, I may not even work on my novel while I'm away."

"Then why—"

"I don't know whether I can explain this so that you or anyone else can understand, Connie, but I need to get back in touch with myself. You see, immersing myself in all the characters of my stories has almost made me forget who I really am or, more precisely, what I am. I want to find some place where I can be in touch with nature again, where I can experience a revival of body and soul and give a deeper meaning to my life."

"I'm trying to understand you, Austin, but I'm finding it difficult. You're a benevolent, caring man, and your books bring countless hours of reading pleasure to thousands of men and women. Don't you take satisfaction in knowing that?"

"Of course I do. Still, I feel this strong pull to go away for a time. And I want to use a name that's less recognizable than my own, so that no one will connect me with my books. I want to step out of my world for a few weeks, at least."

"You can go as far away as you like, Austin, but don't count on escaping your identity. There are too many of your readers who will recognize you on sight from the picture on your book jackets."

Austin had already thought about that. "I'm going to shave off my beard before I go. No one will connect me with the clean-shaven face I plan to present to the world for the next few weeks. And besides, if you find the right spot for me, I won't likely be mingling with people who might recognize me. I plan to become a recluse, remember? Have you come up with a suitable place?"

"Your criteria put this assignment a bit out of my area of expertise, but I've already put out some requests. We'll just have to wait and see what turns up. What's this new name you plan to assume?"

"How about John Austin? After all, both of those names are really mine, and I have every right to use them. We'll merely omit my last one."

"Let's consider your options," Sandy suggested logically.

Meg hovered over her legal pad while she and Sandy drank coffee at the kitchen table. "I guess it's the schoolteacher in me, but I like to put everything down on paper. Beside the number one, she wrote *Return to New York*. "If I do go back to my old job, I could either sell this place or try to hang on to it for vacations, and then it would be here for me when I eventually retire."

"But that's light-years away," Sandy protested. "You have to plan for the present. I've seen a lot of nice houses run down and deteriorate because their owners left them vacant for long periods of time. Listen, Meg, if you have to return to New York, I will understand, and I'll respect your decision, but just make sure that's what you really want to do. But if that is your choice, I certainly would not recommend leaving this place empty for nine months of the year."

"Of course it's not what I really want to do, but I may be forced to," Meg wailed. "I've gone over and over my budget, but the expenses keep growing by leaps and bounds, and the income is limping along trying to keep up." She was silent for a few moments. She had not yet told Sandy about the preposterous idea that kept nudging its way into her thoughts. But now she had to grasp at straws, and she might as well be frank with her friend. "Sandy, if I decided to rent this place for the summer, could I really get the kind of money you talked about?"

"Meg, you saw the long list of people trying to find summer housing, and you saw the pitifully few rentals we've been able to list. Why, a place like this would be snapped up within a week, but then where would you go? Back to New York for the summer?"

"Well, no, actually I was wondering if I could turn my basement into temporary living quarters—"

"Oh, honey, I'm not so sure we could rent out your basement, but you never know!"

"No, no! I mean I would use the basement. Granted, it wouldn't be a palace, but it does have plumbing and electricity. There's an old sleeper sofa, and my cast-off refrigerator, unless it gives out completely. There's even a telephone extension. About the only thing I'd have to add would be a stove."

"Oh, Meg, I don't know. . . ." Sandy looked skeptical, but then she brightened. "Hey, it would only be for a few weeks, and you could continue working for Mr. Hanson. I may have selfish motives, but I sure like that idea better than seeing you return to New York. Let's go downstairs and take a look."

Sandy followed Meg down the stepping-stones to the basement. "Look! The brook runs right by your entrance!"

Meg laughed. "You sound just like the real estate saleslady that you are!" She pushed open the door, and dank, musty air hit her in the face. "I'd sure have to air the place out. I only come down here to do my laundry."

"Some all-weather carpeting might take some of the dampness out."

"Look, Sandy, if I have to start spending a lot of money to fix this place up, my purpose will be defeated."

"Sometimes we sell a house where the owner wants to install new carpeting. I might be able to beg something for you. And I have a two-burner hot plate you could use for a stove. There's no oven, of course, but you aren't going to have much time this summer to bake anyway."

"I have a crock pot and an electric skillet I could use. I think I could make do temporarily without buying a stove. Actually, living in the basement isn't my greatest concern."

"What do you mean?"

"It's just the idea of having someone else upstairs, some stranger using all of my personal belongings: Gran's Haviland china and her pretty figurines and all the things that keep her alive in my heart. I'm not sure I could handle that. I could box up a lot of things and move them downstairs for the summer, I guess."

"If you start removing the personal touches, you're going to remove a lot of the warmth and charm of this place, and we'd have to reduce the amount of rental you can expect to receive," Sandy said. "If you really want to go through with this plan, then I'd advise you to just bite the bullet and go all the way."

"But what if some of my things get broken?"

"You'll have a security deposit to cover your losses."

"Sandy, you know that no amount of money can replace heirlooms."

"Well, you can't have everything your way, but we can be very picky about tenants. You can specify no children and no pets, but with every restriction you add, just remember that you cut down your chances to rent. Anyway, Meg, I can tell that you have a lot of reservations about this idea. I think you'd better sleep on it first to be very sure you'd be comfortable with your decision. If you sign a lease for three months, you have to live with it."

"You're right, Sandy. Let me think about this tonight. Maybe by morning God will have helped me decide on a clear picture of what I should do."

"Whatever you decide, you know that you can count on me to help."

"I know, and you have no idea how much that means to me, Sandy."

Chapter 5

Meg arrived at her desk on Tuesday morning to discover that her red rose had been replaced with a fresh yellow one, and beside it was an envelope bearing her name. She tore it open and pulled out a card. *Welcome to the Hanson Realty Family.* The card was signed by the each member of the office staff plus one name she didn't recognize.

"The cleaning lady," Sandy explained, passing Meg's desk on the way to her work cubicle. "We really are like one big happy family here, and everyone wants to make sure that you know you're appreciated!"

Meg folded the card and put it in her purse. That sweet gesture was going to make it twice as hard to tell them all that she would be leaving as soon as a replacement could be found.

She had wrestled with her decision all through the long night. Sleeping fitfully, she had dreamed of wild children streaking through her house, leaving a trail of broken china and crystal in their wake, and of dogs jumping on her beds and chewing on her curtains, infesting the carpet with their fleas. By the time her alarm sounded at early dawn, she knew with an absolute certainty that she would never let strangers inhabit her home, not even if it meant she had to work in New York for the next twenty years!

She felt guilty about leaving her new job, but she would need these three months of summer to sort through and pack her belongings and make all the necessary arrangements to move back to New York. She could postpone until fall the decision on whether to keep or sell her home.

"Good morning. Hanson Realty. How may I direct your call?" Her day began just as it had the day before, with the phone ringing nonstop throughout the morning and clients entering the office in a steady parade. Mr. Hanson passed her desk once, and she tried to ask if he could schedule a meeting with her, but the phone rang again before she could catch him. Perhaps she could have a word with him during the noon hour. She had no appetite for lunch today, anyway.

"Meg, look at this!" Sandy was breathless as she rushed up to Meg's desk, midmorning, waving a sheet of paper in her hand. "You won't believe what just came in on our fax machine. I think this must be God's answer to our prayers."

Meg had little interest in messages that came over the fax machine today, but she did not want to hurt Sandy's feelings, especially after all that Sandy had done to try to help her. She tried to sound excited. "What is it? Tell me?"

"Your problem! It may be solved! Listen to this: 'Single, professional man, desires quiet, comfortable rental in secluded area. Excellent references.' Don't you see, Meg? It's a direct answer to our prayers!"

"Oh, Sandy, I'm not sure. I–I don't think—"

"No, really, Meg. I'm serious. It's like a miracle. Do you have any idea how unusual it is to receive a request like this? Almost all of our summer renters are families. Just imagine your good fortune if you could rent your house to a single man. He's probably a doctor or a lawyer, and you won't even need to worry about your grandmother's china; he'll probably never cook. He'll either eat out or buy TV dinners. The minute this came over the wire, I knew it was meant for you."

"But a bachelor! He's probably looking for a place where he can stage wild parties. There's no telling what he would bring in."

"Trust me, Meg. The ones who are looking for places to stage wild parties don't come to our remote area. They seek out the big cities where they can find exciting nightlife. About the most exciting thing that happens around here is 'Pickin' on the Square' on Saturday nights. Does that sound like a wild orgy to you?"

"I guess you're right. I just can't imagine why a doctor or a lawyer would want to spend three months in my little house when he could choose a modern condo with maid service. He must have something in mind that we don't know about."

"He probably needs to escape from the pressures of his professional life! Already I find myself feeling sorry for the poor man! You'd really be performing an act of mercy if you offered him a few weeks of rest and relaxation."

Meg thought that Sandy was laying it on a little heavy, in typical salesperson style, but she did give the matter some further consideration. "Since you put it that way, you make it hard to refuse. But, Sandy, I had almost made up my mind not to—"

"Don't let me persuade you to do something you don't want to do, Meg. I know several homeowners who will jump at the chance to find a renter of this caliber, but I wanted to give you the first shot. But of course, if you're not sure. . ."

Sandy let her sentence trail off into thin air, and Meg felt the mercury dropping in her voice. She knew that Sandy was disappointed. "Just give me a little time to think about it, Sandy. You've sprung this on me rather suddenly. But honestly, I do appreciate what you're trying to do for me."

Sandy was not so easily pacified. "I need to fax a reply to this request before some other agency beats me to a commission. Think about it, certainly, but if you want me to offer your place to this customer, you'd better let me know within the hour." She spun on her heels and headed back to her office.

Meg's head was already splitting from stress and lack of sleep, and now her heart grew heavy as she feared she had just burst the bubble of one of her most loyal friends. She thanked God that it was almost noon and she could escape for an hour of solitude and meditation.

She left her desk two minutes early to avoid making excuses to the lunch bunch and crossed the street to the Courthouse Square. On a green wooden bench beneath a spreading oak tree, she sat and watched squirrels scramble for acorns scattered across the grassy lawn.

Even the squirrels have their homes, she thought, as she watched them carry their treasures up the tree trunks and disappear among the branches. All she wanted was a place to call her own, where she could feel in tune with God's plan for her life. Could Sandy possibly be right? Was this strange man's search really God's answer to her prayers? If so, then why didn't she feel more at peace about it?

After all the efforts Sandy had put into helping her, Meg did not want to confess that she had now changed her mind. Perhaps she could throw in a small stumbling block that would discourage the renter yet still refrain from offending Sandy. The amount that Sandy had suggested she ask for rent seemed exorbitant. Meg could hardly believe that anyone in his right mind would be willing to pay that much for a modest house in an isolated area. If she added another two hundred dollars to the monthly rent, then that should be sufficient to discourage even the most desperate tenant.

Having made that decision, Meg walked back to the office and settled herself back at her desk. Just as Mr. Hanson had predicted, the telephone was quiet for a change.

When Sandy came back from lunch, she stopped by Meg's desk. "When you didn't show up for lunch, I was worried about you. Are you okay, Meg?" Genuine concern was spread across her face, and Meg was ashamed that she had thought their friendship could not span a difference of opinion.

"I'm sorry. I should have told you. I needed to get away by myself for a few minutes, to think things through."

"If you're not ready to make a decision yet, don't rush into one. If this tenant doesn't work out for you, perhaps another one will. Or maybe you'll decide the role of landlord is not for you. Whatever you decide, Meg, I'll help you get through it."

Sandy's words filled Meg with shame about her earlier plan to raise the rent. Why, that plan was nothing more than plain deceit, the one characteristic that Meg could never tolerate in others. *You're just like your father,* her mother had often told her, but that had seemed to Meg like the pot calling the kettle black! Today she was acting a little like both of them.

Meg looked up and met the steady eyes of her loyal friend and neighbor. The words came tumbling out of her mouth as though they had a life of their own. "I've decided to offer the place to your client, Sandy. One thing, though, I won't negotiate the rent. If he takes it on my terms, then I'll have to agree with you that it is meant to be, but if he has any reservations, then you can look for another place for him. In that case, I'll remove my house from the market and take it as a sign that I should return to New York."

Sandy gave her a long, steady look. "Fair enough, if you're sure that's what you want to do. I'll send the fax out right away. If he accepts the lease, I'll help you fix up your basement, but if he doesn't, I'll come up the hill and help you start packing."

The phone began to ring again, and Meg watched Sandy disappear down the hall as she lifted the receiver and put a smile in her voice. "Good afternoon. Hanson Realty. How may I direct your call?"

Chapter 6

Thank goodness it isn't raining," Meg said, eyeing the contents of her basement spread across the backyard.

"We'll have everything in place before dark," Jim Goodman promised. "You and Sandy just keep bringing out the sandwiches and iced tea, and leave the rest to us."

In addition to an adequate supply of all-weather carpeting, Sandy had procured a shabby but clean recliner and a small Formica dinette set, all remnants of recent real estate makeovers. And she had assembled a crew, headed by her husband and rounded out by fellow church members, to move Meg's washer, dryer, and refrigerator outside and lay the carpeting on the concrete basement floor.

The minister's wife had salvaged some cotton curtains from the boxes accumulating for the church's upcoming annual rummage sale. She had washed, starched, and pressed them before bringing them to hang in Meg's windows.

"I have some brownies in the oven," Meg said, "and I need to put on a fresh pot of coffee for the workers. I wish there was more I could do to show my appreciation for all this help."

Sandy followed her into the kitchen. "Your neighbors would be quick to tell you that this is the call of the Carolina hills," Sandy said. "Whenever there's a need among us, our people always pitch in together to help. You'll have ample opportunity to respond to that call yourself as time goes by, just as you have in the past."

"I guess that's just one of the reasons I'm determined to make this place my permanent home."

"Let's set up the food on your picnic table down by the brook, and then we can come back inside and start packing your clothes. We'll need to move them downstairs as soon as the workmen finish your apartment."

"My apartment! That makes it seem so final," Meg lamented, casting a wistful glance around her kitchen.

"Did you arrange for a separate phone line?"

"I tried, but the telephone company said an extension was the best I could do for now. I don't think that should be a problem, though. I don't use my phone that often except to talk to you. I'll just have to get used to walking down the hill to your house when I have something to tell you."

"Maybe we can rig up something with tin cans and a string!" Sandy quipped.

"Whatever we rig up is going to have to be done soon. I still can't believe your Mr. Austin is moving in here on Monday, and I won't even be here when he arrives!"

"At least you'll get to eyeball him when he comes in the office to pick up his keys. As the lucky listing agent, I get to bring him out here and show him where everything is. I'll try to give you a full report when I get back."

"Be sure you remind him of the 'no pets rule,' Sandy. And I hope he won't fill up the place with tobacco smoke!"

"You just leave everything to Aunt Sandy! I'll make sure he toes the line. Say, speaking of smoke, does that burning smell have anything to do with what's baking in your oven?"

Meg let out a shriek as she grabbed a potholder and retrieved her pan of well-done chocolate brownies.

Although all her clothes had been moved downstairs to the basement, Meg slept in the familiar comfort of her own bed on Saturday night and again on Sunday, prolonging her separation from home until the last possible moment. When she locked her door on Monday morning to leave for work, she felt as though a part of her body had been severed from her.

Her original misgivings had grown from niggling doubts to full-fledged regret, but there was no turning back now. She had already signed her name to the lease. For the next three months, her home would be in someone else's hands. She was sure that these next three months would be the longest of her life.

At two o'clock in the afternoon, John Austin Bruce stepped through the front door and into the reception area of Hanson Realty Corporation.

Meg looked up from her desk and was momentarily disarmed by his striking appearance. He was well over six feet tall, she decided, with the rugged good looks of a western movie star, but his conservative silk suit and leather briefcase branded him as a wealthy client. "May I help you? Are you here to see Mr. Hanson?"

When he smiled, his brown eyes crinkled at the corners and sparkled under dark, heavy brows that contrasted sharply with his blond hair. "No, I don't believe that was the name I was given." He pulled a card from his pocket. "How about Mrs. Sandra Goodman."

"Who—oh, Sandy. Yes, I'll—" Then, as realization hit her full force, Meg could not seem to control the words coming out of her mouth. "You–you must be. . ."

"John Austin is the name," he answered politely.

Meg pressed Sandy's intercom button. "A Mr. Austin to see you," she said weakly, denying her eyes the satisfaction of curiosity by forcing them to focus on her telephone.

"I'll be right out!"

Sandy emerged from her office and shook hands with her new client. "Welcome to North Carolina, Mr. Austin. Is this your first trip to our state?"

"No, this has long been one of my favorite states, though it has been some time since I've come this way. I'm looking forward to settling in for a short respite."

"My car is in the parking lot. If you'll follow me, I'll take you to see your summer rental. The house we chose for you is several miles outside of Shady Valley in a small, rural area known as Mountain View. If you'll be needing groceries and supplies, we can stop to pick them up on our way out of town. But first let me introduce you to your landlady, Miss Donnelly."

Meg stood on shaky knees and extended her hand. "I hope you'll find my little house comfortable, Mr. Austin."

"Yours?" His arched brows registered surprise. "Why, yes, I hope so, too," he replied before turning his attention back to Sandy. "Well, we'd best be moving on, then. I'd like to get settled in as early as possible." He followed Sandy through the office doorway without a backward glance.

"I drive that little green compact," she told him. "Where are you parked?"

"That's mine," he said, pointing to the big, expensive car he had rented at the airport. "You go ahead, and I'll be right behind you."

Austin had no trouble following Sandy through the narrow, tree-lined streets of the village because there was virtually no traffic. According to Connie, he was arriving before the "busy" season, which even at its peak moved at a snail's pace in the sleepy little village of Shady Valley. So far, Connie's choice was shaping up perfectly for his needs.

Sandy turned into the parking lot of the only supermarket in Shady Valley, and John Austin pulled into the space beside her.

"I won't take very long," he assured her, jumping out of his car. "Now that I'm learning my way around, I can always come back tomorrow. Right now, I'll just buy enough to get me through tonight. I'm anxious to see this place I've rented."

"I'll just wait for you by the door," Sandy said. "I'll step inside where it's cool, but take all the time you need. I live in the Mountain View area myself, and I can tell you that this is the closest store."

"How many people live in the area?" Austin asked uneasily, as they entered the store. "I understood that my house was in an isolated location."

"Oh, it is, believe me! There are probably a hundred or so houses in the area we refer to as Mountain View, but they're scattered all through the mountains. You won't see many of them during your stay, unless you make a real effort to go looking for them."

Somewhat mollified, Austin moved to the dairy case and picked up a gallon of milk and a carton of cottage cheese. He selected a few more items from the grocery shelves and moved into the checkout lane.

After he paid for his groceries, he found Sandy waiting for him by the entrance, just as she had promised. "That didn't take long. If you're sure that's all you need, then let's get started, and I'll lead you to your castle."

Austin enjoyed the drive along the mountain highway. He turned off his air-conditioner and rolled down his windows in order to smell the wildflowers that grew in profusion along the roadside. Their fragrance floated in the crisp mountain air, and Austin filled his lungs with their gentle perfume.

He tried to avoid bumps and holes in the road in order to protect his computer and printer, along with his unfinished manuscript, which were packed in boxes on the backseat. He was anxious to set up and test his computer to make sure it had escaped damage on the plane. But damage was not likely because he had packed and padded everything carefully before he left home.

Sandy's car turned off the highway onto a narrow dirt and gravel road, and Austin followed her. Snaking up the mountainside, the rented car's engine roared as if boasting of its mighty power.

Observing the dense woods all around him, Austin was forced to agree that this was certainly an isolated area. They passed few houses on their way up the mountain road.

Finally, Sandy's car came to a halt, and she gestured toward a small, yellow cottage. Austin pulled his car into the driveway and killed the engine. He could hardly believe his good fortune. Flowers peppered the yard with brilliant color. Squirrels chased each other across the grass, and birds swooped low from the branches above to claim a meal from the many bird feeders scattered about the property. Austin felt that he had arrived in paradise, and best of all, the closest neighbor appeared to be at least a half mile away. "This is wonderful!" he exclaimed, climbing the back porch steps. "Just what I need to finish up my. . .my summer!" He was going to have to remember to watch his tongue!

"Wait until you step inside," Sandy said, opening the kitchen door and leading him through the rooms and onto the redwood deck that spanned the entire width of the house.

Austin did not try to conceal his pleasure. "Mrs. Goodman, I don't know how—"

"Please, if we're going to be neighbors for three months, just call me Sandy."

"Sandy it is, then," he said, extending his hand. "And I'm just plain Aus—uh, John. Anyway, Sandy, thanks for everything. I'm sure I'll be very comfortable here."

"Here's my card in case you think of something else you need." Sandy moved toward the door, and Austin followed her back through the house to the back porch. "I'm going back to Shady Valley now to do my weekly grocery shopping, but I only live half a mile away, so don't hesitate to call if you need help with anything. My Jim is a real handyman."

"Thanks, but this place has everything I could possibly need. I just want some time apart, a place where I can be alone, and you've certainly provided me with complete isolation."

"Oh! Oh, my!" Sandy's face paled before the color began to rise in her cheeks. "Uh, John, there is one thing I forgot to mention. I–I'm sure you'll be able to enjoy complete privacy, but I think you should know that. . ."

❧

For the rest of the day, Meg had trouble keeping her mind on her work. Twice she gave callers the wrong extension, and once she forgot to offer coffee to a client waiting to see Mr. Hanson.

When Sandy had not returned to the office by quitting time, Meg wondered if she had encountered a problem with the house. Somehow, she just could not picture that tall, handsome man in the silk suit feeling comfortable in her cozy little cottage. Perhaps the accommodations had proven too simple for Mr. Austin's taste after all. Maybe he had changed his mind after seeing what an ordinary place he had contracted for. The furnishings that she thought of as quaint and charming would probably appear humble and plain to a man of Mr. Austin's worldly style.

Several of the real estate agents were still working with their clients when Meg locked the front door of the office and straightened her desk. She was anxious to get home and see what surprises this life God had given her held for today. She was fast becoming accustomed to expecting the unexpected!

Meg needed to pick up a quart of milk and a loaf of bread, but she decided to skip the supermarket in her eagerness to head up the hill toward home. Her anxieties mounted with each passing mile. First she would stop at Sandy's house to get a report on her tenant in order to have some idea of what to expect when she arrived at home.

But Sandy's car was not in her driveway. Meg remembered then that Sandy always did her weekly marketing on Monday afternoon. She and Sandy had both planned to buy groceries after work. Should she stay around and wait for her friend to return, or should she drive on up the mountain and see if her new tenant had settled in? She decided on the latter.

Her first shock came when she turned in to park on the gravel grade beside her house and saw that her renter's monstrous car was right in the middle of her two small parking spaces, with hardly enough room on either side to park even a bicycle. This would never do! But even if she asked him to pull over to one side, the size of his car would still take up two-thirds of her parking area. Her only alternative was to leave her own car across the dirt road on a narrow, slanted ledge.

She settled her car in what she considered a rather precarious position and slid across the seat to climb out on the passenger's side. She smoothed out her slim skirt and hobbled across the rocky road with as much dignity as she could muster before ascending her back steps and approaching the kitchen door.

She knocked sharply and waited. When there was no response, she tried again. At last, the back door opened partway and Mr. Austin peered through the crack. "Oh, it's you, Mrs. Donnelly. You'll have to excuse me. I was catching a little nap after my long trip. Was there something you wanted to see me about?"

"Yes. That is, no, never mind." Seeing him there in his terry robe, his hair tousled and his eyes red from lack of sleep, she knew that she had woken him, and she was immediately repentant. "I'm so sorry that I disturbed your nap. I–I just wanted to make sure that you have everything that you need."

"My needs at the moment are very few, Mrs. Donnelly. Nothing a good night's sleep won't take care of. Thank you for inquiring."

"Just for the record, Mr. Austin, the name is *Miss* Donnelly, but Meg suits me better."

"Then Meg it shall be from here on out. And I'm John. And now, Meg, if you'll excuse me. . ."

"Of course," Meg said, backing away from the door. "I'm sorry—" But she did not finish her sentence because he had already closed the door. She had said nothing about the car, but that would have to wait until tomorrow. She certainly couldn't ask him to get dressed to move it, and besides, there was no other place for him to park. She'd have to think of something.

She descended the steps to her new living quarters and unlocked her door. She lingered outside for a few minutes to listen to the murmur of the brook and the songs of the birds. She was not in a hurry to go inside, but at last she took a deep breath and stepped over the threshold.

This would be her home for the next three months, so she'd better learn to like it. She tried to be optimistic as she surveyed her surroundings. The men who laid the carpet had done an excellent job. The bilious green color would not have been her choice, but, hey, this floor covering was given to her and even installed without cost, and it felt much cozier than the cold, bare cement.

Meg sank down in the lounge chair and felt a spring press against her backbone. Perhaps the addition of a couple of sofa pillows would take care of that.

The refrigerator was humming and the floor was dry. The freshly laundered curtains hung at the windows and lifted some of the dreariness from the room. Living in this place would not be so bad on a temporary basis. She repeated that sentence to herself twice and tried hard to believe it.

She should have stopped at the grocery store. What would she fix for supper? She examined the cupboard above her washing machine where she usually kept only laundry detergents and bleach, but where now she had stocked a meager supply of canned goods. She pulled down a can of vegetable soup, but was suddenly hit with the revolting revelation that she had neglected to buy herself a can opener. She would take care of that tomorrow when she went back into town to buy groceries.

She looked in the refrigerator and saw a plate of sandwiches left over from the workday picnic two days ago, and a plastic carton containing the remains of her over-cooked brownies. Not a feast by anyone's standards, but at least she would not starve before morning. She put a pan of water on the hot plate for a cup of instant coffee. Later she would relax in a tub of nice, warm bubbles, and—but then she remembered that she did not have a bathtub downstairs. She would have to settle for a shower.

The anxieties of this day had tired Meg more than physical labor ever could, and she was eager to make up her sofa bed and flop down for a good night's sleep. She washed her few dishes in the sink that had previously been used only to rinse laundry, took a quick shower, and unfolded the couch. She set her alarm clock for six-thirty and stretched out on her unfamiliar bed, determined to ignore its lumps and bumps.

Outside, the birds had finished their songs, and only the croaking frogs broke through the silence of the dark, starry night. A golden half-moon beamed a stream of pale light through the window, and Meg thanked God for sending her a plan that would allow her to keep her house and remain in Mountain View.

Chapter 7

John Austin Bruce was awake before first light. He took his coffee out onto the redwood deck and breathed deeply of the clean mountain air. His eyes spanned the treetops and the misty mountains beyond, and he knew at once that he had made the right choice in coming here to this halcyon place. Not even in the magical words of his fertile imagination could he have designed a more perfect spot.

Except for the worrisome lady downstairs, there was no one within shouting distance to disrupt his solitude. Here midst the silent mountains he would be able to write without interruption. This was exactly the kind of place he had hoped to find. Well, *almost* exactly.

Connie had neglected to tell him that his landlady would be living right under the very same roof. He had almost backed out of the deal when Sandy Goodman had explained the strange arrangement to him. But then Sandy had hastened to assure him that Mrs.—*Meg*—would be working every day during the week, and that she had no children, no pets, and no loud parties. He would hardly know she was there, Sandy promised.

If this Meg person proved to be a problem, he would simply have to explain to her that he had come here to find three months of solitude, and although he was generally a sociable fellow, at the present time, visits and interruptions were not welcome.

Granted, she was a pretty woman in a refreshing sort of way. The brilliance of her clear blue eyes was accentuated by glossy brown hair that framed the fine, delicate features of her face. She had a wholesome, fresh-scrubbed look that he seldom saw among the women in his social set, and when she smiled, which occasion seemed to be a rarity, her whole countenance became illuminated. He would study her features more carefully next time they met and consider trying to assign them to the beautiful protagonist in his latest novel.

He had planned the luxury of a short hiatus from his writing, but already he could feel his creative juices beginning to flow. Funny what a change of air and scenery could do for the human mind. He booted up his computer and began to write a description of Meg Donnelly as he remembered her. He wanted to get this down on paper before his mind galloped off in another direction. He tapped out two descriptive pages before he turned on his printer and transferred the words from his computer screen to paper.

Although Meg had gone to bed early, the unfamiliarity of her surroundings and the uncertainties in her mind worked to make her night less than restful. It was long after midnight before she lapsed into a deep and dreamless sleep.

Just after dawn, she was awakened by a strange sound, alarming at first, and then just plain annoying. Surely the road graders would not be at work so early! She looked at her clock. *Half past five!* No sensible person would be up and about at this hour. She peered out the window, and seeing nothing, she opened her door a crack, but even the birds and squirrels were still sleeping. At last she pinpointed the source of the noise. It was coming from directly above her, out of her very own house!

What could John Austin possibly be doing to create such a noise at five-thirty in the morning? The noise sounded like—rather like the printers in the office of Hanson Realty when they ground out the listings and reports. But that was impossible, because she did not have a printer in her house. Could one of her appliances be making such a noise? If so, she should check on it immediately to make sure there was no fire hazard. John Austin would not like her waking him up a second time, but surely he would see the necessity when she explained her concern. How could he sleep with all that noise in his ears, anyway?

She slid her feet into plastic thongs and wrapped herself in a corduroy robe before she ran up the stairs and across the back porch.

A light was on in the kitchen, and through the window she could see John sitting at the kitchen table, his back to her, bent over something that looked like a laptop computer. And sure enough, a printer similar to the ones at Hanson Realty was spitting out pages of printed material right there in her kitchen.

She raised her hand to knock, but then thought better of it. Now that she knew the source of the irritating noise, there was no need to come in contact with her tenant at this outrageously early hour. Fuming, she went back downstairs, took off her robe, and went back to bed.

Meg tried to go back to sleep, but with the persistent noise grinding just above her head, she found it impossible. She would have to speak to John about that later in the day. She buried her head beneath her pillow to block out the noise and tried to catch another half hour of much-needed rest.

She was still awake when the alarm went off. Wearily, she dragged her aching bones from the bed and selected her clothes for the day. While she dressed, she rehearsed what she would say to Mr. John Austin when she saw him. He was supposed to be on vacation, wasn't he? Then she could see no reason why he should rise so early, but if he did insist upon getting up at daybreak, then he would have to do so quietly. As a working woman, she needed her sleep.

She put a pan of water on the hot plate for her coffee and poured the last of her milk over a bowl of cold cereal. Just as she sat down at the table, her telephone rang. She knew that it would ring upstairs, too. Had Sandy told John about the shared phone? She waited for three rings to make sure he hadn't answered it. She picked up the receiver, but before she had time to speak, she heard his voice on the line. "Hello?"

She waited just long enough to determine that the call was not for her. A woman's voice came over the wire. "Austin?"

"Ramona!"

Meg eased the receiver back onto its cradle. This could get to be very annoying! John Austin had been in residence for less than twenty-four hours, and already women were calling him on the telephone. In one short day he had disrupted her life completely. She would never be able to tolerate this for three long months.

Meg was mildly curious about his call. Oddly, the woman had called him by his last name, but she had not preceded it by Mister. And he had called her "Ramona." This Ramona person must know John Austin pretty well if she called him long distance at seven o'clock in the morning. Well, that was not any of Meg's business, and she certainly had no interest in his personal life. No interest whatsoever!

She finished her breakfast and tidied her small apartment. In such close quarters, everything must be kept in perfect order or else the whole place would be utter chaos.

Meg put on her makeup in the tiny bathroom illuminated by a bare lightbulb dangling on a cord, with only a cheap twelve-by-twelve mirror to guide her. Upstairs, John Austin was probably shaving in her airy, well-illuminated bathroom, his actions reflected in a clear mirror that covered half the wall. She could hear his footsteps as he padded barefoot back and forth across the floor above her.

She *must* have a talk with him, and soon. There were several things that needed to be understood between them if they were to share a house for the entire summer. Already she was running late, and there was no time for such a talk this morning. She would stop in to see him as soon as she came home this evening. They might as well come to an understanding from the very beginning.

Chapter 8

Austin was surprised when he looked at the kitchen clock and realized that he had worked through half the morning. He smiled, thinking of that hiatus he had promised himself. His mind was like a pump that had to be primed, but once he had coaxed a trickle, it continued to gush out fresh ideas from the wellspring of his imagination. He had started by writing a vivid description of his protagonist and had ended by completing half of a chapter!

He was pleased with himself. The old well had not run dry after all. It just needed to be primed, and the beautiful North Carolina mountains were certainly the right place to come for that.

He took his Bible onto the deck for a few moments of quiet study and meditation before he began his day in earnest. Accompanied by the pleasant sounds of the rippling stream below, his thoughts turned to God, and John Austin Bruce found a peace that had eluded him in recent weeks.

Since Meg knew that she would find it difficult to prepare proper meals in her new living quarters, she ordered the blue plate special for her noonday meal. Between bites, she related to Sandy the trials she had encountered on the first day of her experience as a landlady. She ended by saying, "I can already see trouble ahead. John Austin is simply an impossible man, and I just don't see how I can continue in this arrangement for three whole months!"

Across the table from her, Sandy studied her friend with some concern. "Meg, I don't think you even realize this, but you're carrying around a load of uncharacteristic resentment on your shoulders, and that can get to be a real burden."

Meg bristled and hastened to defend herself. "No, I'm not, Sandy. I know that this rental arrangement is making it possible for me to stay here in Mountain View and keep my house. Really, I appreciate the man. It's just that we need to set a few things straight from the get-go."

Sandy gentled her tone. "Would you like me to come with you to talk to him this afternoon?"

"Oh, Sandy, would you?" But as quickly as the words left her mouth,

Meg retracted them. "No, I need to face him myself, one-on-one. After all, we're two mature adults, and we should be able to work out our problems in a civilized manner."

"Well, I need to tell you that he was less than thrilled when he learned that his landlady was living under his roof—or under his *floor*, to be more precise. He was most emphatic in telling me that privacy is his first priority, and I assured him that he would hardly know that you were there."

"And that will be true, once we get things settled between us. Don't worry, Sandy, I won't scare him away. I'll let him know that I intend to respect his privacy, and of course, I will expect the same consideration from him."

The women cut their lunch hour short in order to return to work early. The office had been buzzing with activity all morning. Now that school was out, families were flocking to the mountains, just as Sandy had predicted, and Meg had her hands full answering the phone and keeping order in the reception area. She passed out maps and brochures with one hand while she connected calls with the other. At five o'clock, after the doors were locked, it took them an extra hour to serve the customers who were already inside and to empty the office.

At six o'clock, Meg pulled her blue compact car out of the parking lot and tried to plan her meeting with John Austin. Sandy's words kept ringing in her ears. Was it true that she was carrying a heavy load of resentment? And if she was, how long had she been carrying it? Had it sprung from this insane summer rental arrangement, or had it been born long ago at a different time in a different place? These thoughts disturbed her. She knew that she would have to work on them, and she would ask God to help her.

She stopped at the supermarket to get a few things, and in a sudden burst of neighborliness, she purchased a warm apple pie from the bakery. She would take this to John Austin when she met with him, to make sure her visit didn't turn into a confrontation. Bakery pies weren't the same as homemade ones, but with no oven in her basement apartment, this was the best that she could provide. To a bachelor who was cooking for himself, even a bakery pie would probably be a welcome treat.

She had talked herself into feeling better about the whole summer arrangement until she drove up the mountain road to her home and remembered that she would have to park on the narrow shoulder across from her drive. Her temper began to rise again, but recalling Sandy's words, she swallowed her anger, whispered a prayer, and tried to hum a tune.

She carried her bags of groceries down the steep incline to her basement apartment and put them away before she took her pie in hand and started up the back steps. She had tried dozens of times to decide how she would begin their conversation, but so far, none of her ideas seemed quite right. Her knees were shaking when she knocked on her own back door.

She could hear a chair scrape across the floor and then footsteps coming her way. John opened the door partway and looked down at her from his towering height. She had almost forgotten how handsome he was, but today he was not smiling. "Yes?"

That wasn't exactly the warm welcome she had hoped for, but she forged ahead. "Mr. Austin—John—I. . .I thought since you just moved in, you might like an apple pie for your dessert."

He stood looking through the partially opened door for a long moment, but at last, he pushed it wide and, reaching for the pie, gave her a polite smile. "Thank you, uh, Meg. This is very thoughtful of you. I'm sorry that I can't invite you to come in just now and share it with me, but you see, I am rather busy at the moment, and—"

"I don't mean to intrude on your privacy, John, but there are a few things we need to talk about. I promise not to take too much of your time, and once we get a few things settled, I'll try not to bother you again."

She could see his reluctance. "If this is not a good time, I could come back later," she offered. "Say in about an hour?"

"All right," he agreed, with a noticeable lack of enthusiasm.

Meg could think of no way to immediately prolong the visit she had anticipated all day. She stepped back onto the porch and turned to go. "I'll be back in an hour, then."

She was halfway down the stairs when she heard him call to her, "Thank you for the pie, Meg. Thank you very much."

Seated at her small dinette set, Meg ate a tuna fish sandwich and drank a glass of milk. Having slept only a few hours the night before, she felt drained of all energy. If only she had been able to have that talk with her tenant earlier, she could have been done with it by now! It was already eight o'clock. The way things were going, she was not likely to get to bed before ten tonight. Her life had certainly been turned upside down since the arrival of Mr. John Austin. Did he have any idea the amount of trouble he was causing for her? Then, as quickly as she had conjured that thought, she remembered Sandy's earlier admonition, and Meg had to admit that Sandy was probably right. Changing her attitude toward this situation was certainly going to take a lot of prayer and hard work on her part. Was God testing her?

Directly above her, Austin Bruce was doing a bit of soul searching, himself. He realized that he had been downright rude to the lady, and rudeness was not his style. This talk she was proposing would probably turn out to be a good thing after all; a time to clear the air for both of them. Whatever it was she expected of him, he could not imagine. At least this talk would give him an opportunity to explain that he had business matters which required his full attention and that he had no desire to indulge in any type of social exchange.

He began to cover his work so that the pages of his manuscript would not be revealed when she visited him. So far, everyone had accepted him as simply *John Austin.* Although his face appeared on the back cover of several of his recent books, he thought it unlikely that anyone would make a connection between the bearded image of Austin Bruce, the author, and John Austin, the clean-shaven man who was spending his summer in a modest mountain cottage.

He hoped that he could get Meg to smile for him when she returned. He had managed to capture her lovely likeness in words, all of her fine features except for her winsome smile. But her smile, on the rare occasions when he had witnessed it, possessed an appeal that seemed to elude description when he tried to transfer it to paper. Was she always so unhappy, or was it simply the effect he had on her?

He stacked his dinner dishes in the sink and started a pot of coffee in the automatic drip machine. He used a special blend of coffee beans that he had brought along in his suitcase all the way from Florida, because he was rather fussy when it came to a good cup of coffee.

He picked up wads of discarded manuscript, which he had rejected and tossed on the floor throughout the day, and transferred them to the wastebasket. He retrieved his nylon windbreaker from the back of a chair and threw it into the bedroom, and he closed the door on his unmade bed. By the time the hour had passed, he had restored the kitchen to reasonable order.

Meg was prompt. "John? May I come in?" How strange it seemed to be asking permission to enter her own home!

"Please do," John invited, holding the door wide for her this time. "I've just made a pot of coffee. Would you like a cup?"

After drinking nothing but instant coffee made on her hot plate, the aroma of fresh-brewed coffee smelled heavenly to Meg, but she tempered her enthusiasm. "That would be very nice, thank you."

John served the coffee in Meg's best china cups, the ones she usually saved for special occasions. She had to bite her tongue to keep from suggesting that he use her everyday dishes. She watched him cut generous wedges of apple pie and place them on two thin Haviland dessert plates. "Thank you," she said, giving him a tight smile.

When he was seated and sipping his coffee, she began. "First, I want to explain about the telephone. I'm sorry that I have only been able to get one line, with an extension in my apartment downstairs. However, I want you to feel that the phone is yours. I will keep my calls to a minimum, and I will answer only after the third ring when I'll assume that you are not available."

"But what if the caller asks to speak to you?"

Meg thought for a moment. "If that happens," she said, "Use the broom handle to knock three times on the floor. I'll hear you and pick up the extension."

"Fair enough. And if you answer a call that is meant for me, will you do the same? That is, will you knock on your ceiling three times so that I will hear you?"

"Yes, that should work. I don't think you will find this an inconvenience, because I don't expect to be receiving many calls." Meg lifted her cup to her lips and savored the full-bodied flavor of coffee, a gourmet blend, she would guess. And drinking from the delicate, gold-rimmed cup seemed to enrich the taste and heighten her enjoyment.

"Now, what else was there that you wanted us to discuss?" Austin was giving her an opportunity to say everything that was on her mind before he began to tell her of his own concerns.

Meg decided to delay a discussion of parking the cars until she could come up with a workable solution. As unsatisfactory as it was to park her small car on the narrow, roadside ledge, parking her tenant's huge sedan there would be impossible. Instead, she turned her attention to his computer and printer positioned on one side of her solid maple dining table. "John, do you suppose it would be asking too much to have you put a towel beneath your equipment in order to protect my table? You see, I would hate to have it scratched, and—"

"Of course. I should have thought of that myself. I'll take care of it at once. Now, what else do we need to talk about?"

"Well, uh. . ." Here she hesitated. This might prove to be a little stickier.

"Go ahead," he urged. "We want to get everything out on the table."

"It's just that you seem to get up so early, and, well, I do need my sleep, and—"

"Now, look here, Miss Donnelly!"

Meg took it as a bad sign that he had reverted to using her last name. She saw the color in his cheeks intensify.

He struggled for patience. "I will abide by the strange telephone answering system, and I will put down not one but two towels to make sure your table does not get a single scratch, but Miss Donnelly, I refuse to adjust my work schedule to yours, and if that poses a problem for you, then one of us will have to find another place to spend the summer."

"Really, Mr. Austin! I hardly think we need to get so worked up about this thing. I am quite willing to make certain adjustments, but all I am asking is that you show a little consideration by keeping the noise level down until seven o'clock."

"Is there anything more?" he inquired tersely, without issuing any promises.

"Just that—would you mind terribly if I had another cup of that coffee before I leave? It's very good."

Austin rose and filled her cup. "Now, may I have a turn? Because I have a request of my own."

"Certainly," she said, trying to steady the hand that raised her coffee cup to her lips. "What can I do for you?"

"Nothing, really." He noted the questioning arch of her eyebrows. "I mean that literally. Nothing. I need nothing except to be left alone."

Meg sloshed coffee on the table in her haste to rise to her feet. "Well, please excuse me," she said, moving toward the door. "You will not be bothered by my presence again, Mr. Austin."

He stepped in front of her, barring her path to the door. "Meg, wait. Don't leave in anger. I'm sorry to be so blunt. Just let me explain—"

"There's no need—" she began.

"But I really want to. Please sit down and hear me out."

Meg stopped to hear what he had to say, but she did not sit down.

"I brought some important work with me when I came here; work that must be finished before I leave. As much as I would enjoy getting to know you better, I simply cannot afford the luxury of leisure until my work is finished. I shouldn't have sounded so unfriendly, because I do appreciate your kindness, but I simply don't know any pleasant way to state my case."

Meg's anger brought a rush of blood to her face. She struggled to find a smart retort that would let this egotistical man know that her own schedule was as busy as his, and that she, too, would welcome a pact of privacy.

But before she could speak, the silence of the night was broken by a loud crash as a brick sailed through the kitchen window, narrowly missing her shoulder and sending a spray of splintering glass across the floor.

Meg gave a sharp cry and jumped back, but John bounded out the kitchen door in time to see the back end of a blue pickup truck as it spun off and disappeared into the darkness.

"Are you all right, Meg?" he asked, coming back into the kitchen and moving to her side. "Did any of that glass cut you?"

Too shaken to answer, she shook her head. She was trembling, and John put an arm around her shoulders. "Come sit down in the living room. What do you suppose that was all about?"

"I can't imagine," she said, but her teeth were chattering and a chill swept through her body.

"I tried to get a license plate number, but I was too late. Look, you sit right here while I fix you a cup of hot tea. First I'm going to put in a call to the sheriff. Then I'm going to clean up some of that glass." He pulled a crocheted afghan from the back of the couch and wrapped it around her. Then he went back into the kitchen, stepping carefully to avoid the shards of glass.

After calling and giving directions to the dispatcher in the sheriff's office, Austin turned his attention to the mess surrounding him. The brick had made an ugly dent in Meg's vinyl floor covering. Wanting to preserve any possible fingerprints, he used a paper towel to gingerly lift the brick by its edges and place it on the counter, and when he did, he saw the note taped to the underside. In crude printing, the words said, "I don't get mad. I just get even." And, of course, it was unsigned.

By the time John cleared the floor of glass, the water in the kettle was boiling. He made a mug of strong tea and carried it to the living room. He was happy to note that the color was returning to Meg's face, and she looked much more in control. "Here, drink this. It will make you feel better."

He set her mug on the coffee table in front of her and tried to make some sense of what had just happened. He decided not to tell her about the note on the brick until after the law enforcement officers arrived. "Have you any idea who might be responsible for such a thing?"

Meg looked at him and slowly nodded. "I have a pretty good idea."

All earlier hostilities were now completely forgotten by them both, as were their individual plans to spend a quiet evening alone. The same strange rental scheme that had formed a wedge of controversy between them had now drawn them together in a bond of adversity.

Chapter 9

Meg had little doubt as to who was responsible for throwing that brick through her window and to the motive behind the vicious act that could have proven deadly.

When the sheriff and one of his deputies arrived, they confirmed her worst suspicions: Bud McLendon had appeared in court that afternoon and had lost his appeal to have Billy returned to his custody.

"He holds me responsible for that," Meg told them. "He has verbally threatened me before, but I never expected him to do anything like this!"

"Bud drives a blue pickup all right, but that's not sufficient evidence to arrest him. We can't prove anything yet," the sheriff told her, "and we can't justify stationing a man out here on permanent duty. We'll take this brick and the note and have them checked for fingerprints, but until we can prove that McLendon actually committed a crime, we can't lay a finger on him."

"Can't she get a restraining order?" Austin asked.

"Yes, but that seldom has any effect on a man like Bud McLendon. He's mean and vindictive. That man spends more time in jail than he does at home. I'd urge you to be extremely careful until we can come up with enough evidence to arrest the man, Miss Donnelly."

After the two officers left, Austin's gentle kindness to Meg seemed to erase the contentious words that had passed between them earlier. "Don't worry about the window glass. I'll take care of that tomorrow," he told her.

"That's kind of you, John. Just save the receipts and I'll reimburse you for the costs. I think my homeowner's insurance will cover it. I'm just sorry for the inconvenience to you."

"Don't worry about it." He insisted on accompanying her down the stairs to her apartment and waiting until she was safely locked inside before leaving her.

She slept easily that night, finding comfort in the knowledge that John Austin was sharing her house and that he was concerned for her safety.

Bud McLendon was a bully and a coward. Meg thought it unlikely that he would return to cause her further trouble once he heard that the sheriff was on his trail. He would wait until he thought she had lowered her guard before he struck again. And she was glad to hear that poor, young Billy had not been returned to his cruel father's custody.

She did not share the unpleasant incident with Sandy, feeling that the less said about the matter, the better. She took the normal precautions of keeping her eyes and ears open and her doors locked. John had replaced the broken windowpane, and the week passed without further disturbances.

True to their agreement, she and John seldom saw each other in the days that followed. She had become fairly comfortable in her small quarters, and work in the office had settled into a pleasant routine. By Friday afternoon, Meg had almost put her anxieties to rest until she arrived at home, parked her car in the same hazardous location, and started toward her back steps.

She stopped and did a double take when she passed her back porch, because there, curled up on her welcome mat outside the kitchen door was a large, gray cat, sleeping peacefully as though he owned the place.

Hadn't Sandy told John Austin that she did not allow pets? She had made that clear in the beginning. When she moved back into her own quarters in the fall, she did not want to find the place infested with fleas! How dare her tenant break their agreement in such a blatant manner! And how was she supposed to discuss this with him if he did not want to be interrupted?

When she walked up on the porch, she could hear his printer churning out his work. At least, this time he was not asleep. Looking down at the sleeping cat, she hesitated. Perhaps she should wait until she saw John Austin come outside before she approached him about his cat. She was about to turn and leave when she saw something else—something that made her blood boil! A saucer of milk had been placed on the porch, and not just an ordinary saucer! This unwelcome cat had been drinking his milk from her grandmother's beautiful Haviland china!

Without further hesitation, she pounded on the door. "John!"

He met her with a look of alarm. "What is it, Meg? Is someone bothering you again?"

"Yes," she said. "What's bothering me is your cat!"

"*My* cat? I thought he was *your* cat!"

"Do you mean to tell me that this cat you're feeding out of my best china is not even your cat?"

John Austin looked sheepish. "I guess I didn't really stop to consider what dish I used," he admitted. "This cat set up such a howl at my back door that I thought surely he must be yours. He acts like he lives here."

Her temper cooled as she listened to him offering his excuses. In fact, she could not suppress her smile. He looked as vulnerable as a small boy caught with his fingers in the cookie jar. She picked up the fragile saucer that still held traces of milk and handed it to him. "I suppose there was no harm done, and just for the record, I don't dislike cats. In fact, I'm rather fond of them, but I don't own one. I don't know who this cat belongs to."

"My apologies, then. I'll wash the dish, and I promise not to feed him again. When he gets hungry enough, he's sure to return to wherever he came from."

"And I'm sorry that I interrupted your work again," she said graciously. "I know that I promised not to."

"Apology accepted. And now that I've stopped my work anyway, why don't you step in and join me for a cup of that coffee you seemed to enjoy so much?"

"Are you sure I won't be interrupting your work?"

"The coffee is already made, and I need to take a break. We can make it a short one." He held the door open wide, and she stepped over the sleeping cat and into the kitchen.

She noticed that he had padded her dining table with towels beneath his computer and printer. A thick pile of paperwork had accumulated on the tray of his printer, but he hastily turned the top page over so that she could not see what he was working on.

"Let's take this out on the deck," he suggested, pouring coffee into two large, ceramic mugs.

Meg followed him through the living room and out the front door. "This is my favorite place," Meg confessed. "My grandmother and I used to spend hours out here."

As soon as they were comfortably settled on the wicker chairs, two bushy-tailed squirrels joined them. John reached for a jar of peanuts on the table and threw a handful on the floor. "I'm afraid I'm spoiling your squirrels," he said, watching them vie for the treats.

"Now you see why I don't have a cat! I love those cute little critters."

"I think our cat visitor is much too lazy to chase squirrels, but I'll keep an eye out, just in case."

Wind chimes hanging from a corner of the deck caught the late afternoon breeze and tinkled a gentle accompaniment to the soothing sounds of the flowing brook below. The short break stretched into a pleasant hour before Meg realized that she might have overstayed her welcome. Rising suddenly, she flushed and said, "I'm sorry, John. Truly, I only meant to stay for a few minutes!"

"It hardly seems longer than that, Meg. Perhaps—" But, remembering his purpose in choosing this isolated retreat and his earlier resolve to avoid personal contacts, he caught himself short of saying, "Perhaps we can do this again." Instead he said, "Perhaps—the cat will decide to leave by tomorrow."

He moved across the deck to open the front door to the living room for her, but instead, she went down the steep wooden stairs that led to the ground below. "I'll just go down this way," she said with a laugh, "so I won't have to disturb our cat."

Austin leaned over the railing and watched her descend. The breeze lifted her long brown hair, and he noted the graceful curve of her slender neck. She really was lovely, he thought. At another place in another time, he might—but he hurried to return to his computer. He had wasted too much of this day already.

ꙮ

Meg unlocked the door to her apartment and stepped inside. The stale, sultry air was oppressive. She threw open the windows and turned on a small oscillating fan. In contrast, she could visualize John Austin enjoying the fresh mountain air that swept pleasantly through her house upstairs, but she was happy to note that she no longer carried that burden of resentment Sandy had warned her of.

True, she would rather be living upstairs than down here in this cramped, sparsely furnished apartment, but she could now look at the big picture and count John Austin's presence as one of her many blessings. By the time school started again, she would have a nice little nest egg in her savings account. Her tenant would be out of her house and gone!

What she couldn't understand was why that thought no longer seemed to excite her.

Chapter 10

Because she had volunteered to help at the church rummage sale on Saturday morning, Meg had set her alarm to wake early. *But not this early,* she thought dourly when the telephone woke her from a pleasant dream.

She rolled out of bed before she remembered that John Austin was supposed to have the first opportunity to answer incoming calls. She counted two rings and then silence. She pictured John answering, and she could imagine Ramona's voice coming over the line. For some reason that she could not explain, that thought seemed to irritate her. Why, it was only six thirty in the morning! Whatever could that woman be thinking of?

But it was not Ramona after all. Meg heard three sharp raps from the floor upstairs, and a fine sprinkle of chalky, white plaster dust fell from her ceiling and sifted down into her hair. Just as her temper began to rise, she remembered that this was John Austin's signal that the telephone call was for her.

She lifted the receiver from the wall phone. "Hello?"

"Meg, I feel terrible about calling you so early, because I could tell that I woke your renter, but I had to call you."

"It's all right, Sandy. His calls have waked me a few times. What's up? Are you getting ready to help at the big rummage sale today?"

"No, Meg. That's why I'm calling. Beth just called to tell me she's coming home from college for the weekend, and she's bringing two of her friends with her."

"But that's great news, Sandy. I know how much you've missed your daughter since she left for summer semester. What's the problem?"

"No problem, really. I'm thrilled, of course. But this house is a wreck, and I'll need to run into town for extra groceries, and I want to do some baking and cooking before they get in. I want to have everything done in advance so that I'll have time to enjoy them while they're here."

"What time are they coming?"

"They'll be here for lunch! Isn't that just like a nineteen-year-old? If she had warned me yesterday, I'd be all set and ready. As it is, I'm afraid I'll have to beg off helping at the rummage sale."

"That won't be a problem, Sandy. You know we always have tons of help."

"I know that. Otherwise, I'd be there in spite of this unexpected turn of events. I just wanted to explain my situation to you and ask you if you'd mind explaining to the others and taking my rummage to the sale."

"But you already took your things last Wednesday. Don't you remember? We both took our things and stayed to help tag them."

"Yes, but Jim just gave me a pair of shoes he says aren't comfortable. They're good shoes, and they've hardly been worn, but he said he'd rather give them to someone who could use them than have them continue to sit in his closet gathering dust."

"Sure, Sandy. No problem. Want me to stop by and pick them up on my way to the church?"

"No, you don't need to do that, Meg. I'm going to hike up the mountain to pick some blackberries for my pies, and I'll just set them on your back porch."

"Fine. I'll take them along with me when I go, and I'll tell the others why you can't be there. Just have a great time with Beth and her friends. You deserve it!"

Meg was wide awake now, and she did not return to her bed. Instead, she ate a bowl of cornflakes and drank two cups of instant coffee. A piece of toast would be nice, if she had a downstairs toaster.

Meg smoothed her sheets and folded up the sofa bed. She washed her few dishes and returned the bottle of milk to the refrigerator. One advantage to this simple living arrangement was that it required very little housework.

She pulled on a pair of jeans, topped them with a T-shirt, and chose her most comfortable shoes—a pair of faded blue sneakers. She was sure to be on her feet all morning, so she might as well be comfortable.

She was excited about the rummage sale. At their last sale, the ladies of the church had raised over five hundred dollars, and all of it had been clear profit! They hoped to buy an organ for the sanctuary before Christmas, to replace the old upright piano that Mrs. Simpson used each Sunday to accompany the hymns. These same women had cleared nearly two hundred dollars on their bake sale, and the organ fund was steadily edging toward its goal. Hopefully, today's sale would give it a hefty push to the top.

By eight o'clock, Meg was dressed and ready to go. Although the sale would not start until nine, she wanted to arrive early enough to help with the setup.

She locked her apartment door and climbed the stone steps. She almost forgot about Jim's shoes until she passed the back porch and saw them sitting by the kitchen door. She picked them up and looked at them. My! They were nice! Just as Sandy had said, they appeared almost new. It was hard to imagine that Jim could not use them.

The big, gray cat was still comfortably settled on the welcome mat, but Meg saw no bowl to indicate that John was still feeding him. Surely the animal would leave before the day was out.

"Meow!" The cat raised his head and looked hopefully at Meg.

"You poor thing," Meg said, scratching the top of his head with her free hand. "You must be starving. Why don't you go home where you belong?"

Meg carried the shoes to her car and put them in the backseat. She edged her car back onto the roadway and backed into her drive to turn her car around. John Austin's humongous gas guzzler blocked her path and made the task difficult. She had to seesaw back and forth several times before she could change her direction and drive down the mountainside to the asphalt road.

The church was only two miles down the highway, and Meg was one of the first workers to arrive. She set to work at once arranging merchandise on the temporary tables the men had built by placing plywood over sawhorses.

"Where are you putting the men's clothing?" she asked Sara, the young woman who was directing the sale.

"Over there on that second table beneath the oak tree. Did Sandy come with you?"

"No, she had an unexpected call. She won't be here today, but she did send these shoes of Jim's."

"My goodness, they look brand new! Some lucky man will snap those up in a hurry. They look too big for my Neal, or I'd buy them myself."

People began arriving well before the designated hour, lining up to be first to make their selections. Once the sale began, business was booming. The most popular items were children's clothing and toys. The workers bagged merchandise in recycled plastic grocery bags and put the money in a cigar box. Meg was excited to see how fast the money box was filling up.

"How much fer these here shoes?" a man asked, holding up the pair of Jim's shoes that Meg had added to the table.

Meg was about to say, "Five dollars," until she saw the man's destitute appearance. His clothes, though clean, were faded and torn, and his toes protruded from the old brogans he wore. "Two dollars," she said quickly, before anyone else could price them higher.

The man dug a crumpled dollar bill from his overall pocket, and counted out a dollar's worth of small change to make up the difference.

"Thank you," Meg told him. "I'll put these in a bag for you."

"No need, ma'am. I'd jest as soon carry 'em." His eyes reflected a solemn pride that warmed Meg's heart. *Raising money for the organ fund was not the only benevolence realized from these rummage sales,* she thought. They filled another need that was far greater and infinitely more important.

She turned back to serve the next customer. She was busily bagging merchandise when she heard someone call her name. "Hi, Meg! How's it going?"

"Sandy! It's going just great! Just look at this turnout! But what are you doing here? I thought you weren't planning to come today."

"I can't stay," Sandy said. "I just came by to bring Jim's shoes. By the time I made it up to your house, you had already left, so I decided to run them down here myself. Anyway, I wanted to come and bring some of these cookies for the workers." Then, seeing Meg's face blanch and her mouth drop open, Sandy said, "What is it, Meg? What's wrong?"

"Your—Jim's—I mean, the *shoes*."

Sandy held them up. "Oh, these? These are the shoes I told you about. I'll put them here on the table, and maybe somebody will come along and buy them."

"But, what—I mean, whose— Oh, no! Are you telling me you didn't put Jim's shoes on my porch this morning?"

"Well, no, but you don't need to get so upset about it. After all, I did bring them, didn't I?"

"Oh, Sandy! I'm afraid I just sold a perfectly good pair of John Austin's shoes!"

"You what!"

"Well, I didn't mean to, of course, but I saw them on the back porch, and I just assumed. . ."

"Where are they?" Sandy frantically perused the table of men's wear. "We'll have to take them back to him."

"But I can't!" wailed Meg. "I just sold them to a man for two dollars."

"Oh, Meg! You didn't!" But the look on Meg's face defied denial. "Who bought them? We'll have to find him and get them back!"

Meg frantically scanned the crowd, but saw no one who even remotely resembled the man who had purchased the shoes. "Oh, whatever am I going to do? How will I ever explain this to John?"

Sandy picked up the shoes she had placed on the table. "Were they anything like these? Do you think he could wear these?"

Meg knew that her friend was trying to be helpful, so how could she possibly explain that the shoes she had sold were made of finest leather, soft and supple, obviously a very expensive pair. She merely replied, "No, John's were black, and they appeared to be larger than Jim's. I'll just have to go home and tell him exactly what happened and offer to buy him another pair."

"I'm so sorry. Somehow, I feel at least partially responsible. I should never have burdened you with the responsibility of taking Jim's shoes in the first place. Well, here, take these along anyway. Maybe he can make do with them until you can get him another pair."

"It's no one's fault. It was an honest mistake. I just hope I can make John realize that. Anyway, Sandy, just go on and get ready for your guests. This is my problem, and I'll have to work it out."

Austin reread the chapter he had just pulled from his printer, and a satisfied smile spread across his face. At the rate he was going, he would have the final manuscript ready to send to Ramona before the end of the month, well ahead of the schedule he had set for himself.

He had been working for three hours without a break, and now he would stop for a cup of coffee on the deck. This was a treat he looked forward to each morning. The birds and squirrels had become his friends, and the sound of rustling leaves, the melodic tinkling of wind chimes, and the constant sonata of the brook filled him with a quiet reverence.

But first, he'd better bring in his shoes in case it rained. He had polished them before he began working this morning and set them on the porch to dry. He would need them for church tomorrow.

He was not sure where he would go for Sunday worship; there were several options. Initially, he had planned to attend the red brick church that he had spotted when he first arrived in town and drove through the streets of Shady Valley. Located only a block from Courthouse Square, the church appeared to be a smaller version of the one he attended in Florida when he was at home. But then, just yesterday, as he drove along the highway, he had seen a quaint country church, a small wooden structure with a towering steeple. Its warmth and charm seemed irresistible, and he had not been able to shake its image from his mind.

He measured coffee into the pot and filled the tank with water. While his coffee was brewing, he would put away his completed chapter, bring in his shoes, and check on that persistent cat that seemed to have taken up permanent residence on his doorstep.

When he opened his back door, he had to step carefully to avoid coming down on the sleeping cat. "What's the matter with you, boy? Don't you know that you don't live here?"

"Meow!"

"Now, look here, buster! You can't stay. My landlady says 'no cats,' and that means you." He picked up the heavy feline and deposited him gently over the edge of the porch. "Go on home, now. Your family is probably looking for you.

Austin turned to pick up his shoes, and he forgot all about cats when he realized that his shoes were *gone*! He looked over the edge of the porch to see if the cat could have knocked them down, although he knew that this was not a plausible explanation. And certainly the wind could not have blown them away; they were quite heavy and there was very little wind. Could a dog have carried them away? He had not seen a dog around here since he moved in, and besides, the cat would hardly be sleeping so peacefully if a dog had come up on the porch. What else was there to think? That someone came along and stole his best pair of shoes?

He scratched his head in disbelief, as though his eyes must be deceiving him as he scanned every inch of the porch and the surrounding turf a second time.

Hearing the sound of an approaching car, he turned his eyes to the road. When Meg's car rounded the curve, Austin was at least partially relieved, hoping that she might be able to help him solve the mystery. If there was someone in this area with a reputation for thievery, she could surely guess the identity of the guilty party and perhaps help him find his nearly new, custom-made shoes.

Chapter 11

Austin watched Meg park her car and trudge across the backyard toward his porch. Her cheeks were pale and her eyes had a tired look about them that he had never seen in them before. He knew at once that she was ill, and he hated to add to her discomfort by burdening her with his own personal problem. Still, if he was to catch a thief, time was of the essence. He met her at the bottom of the porch steps. "Meg, I have a problem."

"I know," she said, not meeting his eyes. "Can we talk about it?"

There seemed to be some missing pieces to this puzzle. How could she possibly know anything about his problem—unless she was somehow connected to it? Austin sensed that he should move slowly until he could ferret out more of the details. "Won't you come in? I've made fresh coffee."

"No coffee, thanks. Just let me come in and explain everything."

When he led her into the house, he saw that she was trembling. "Go out on the deck. I'll join you there in just a minute."

Meg settled herself on one of the wicker chairs and tried to imagine how she would begin to explain her terrible mistake. Silently, she rehearsed several opening sentences, but none seemed adequate.

Austin pushed through the doorway, carrying a tray with two coffee mugs and two of her best embroidered linen napkins. "Maybe this will make you feel better," he said.

"John—" She faltered, trying to find the right words.

"Meg, does this by any chance have something to do with my missing shoes?"

Meg's eyes filled with tears, and she nodded her head. "John, I'm so sorry."

As she unfolded her story, Austin's face displayed every emotion from anger to sympathy, and even a touch of amusement. He shook his head. "I can't believe this!"

"I'll pay for them," she added hastily. "You can shop for a new pair this afternoon, any kind you choose, and I'll reimburse you for their cost. I know that they were very good shoes."

He seriously doubted that she had any idea just how "good" they actually were. He had no intention of telling her that those shoes were made especially for his feet, at a cost of over two hundred dollars. Instead, he said, "I'd like to get them back. Can't we find the man who bought them and explain what happened?"

"Don't you think I've already thought of that? I described the man to everyone who helped with the sale today, but no one had a clue as to his identity."

"Meg, I'm trying to be reasonable, but I want those shoes back! Perhaps you'll see this man in town, or at the grocery store. Just keep looking for him, please." He tried to control his anger. No amount of rage would get his shoes back, and she did look pitifully embarrassed. "Couldn't you put an ad in the local newspaper?"

"I could try that, but truthfully, I doubt that it would do any good. The man who bought your shoes—well, he did not look like the kind of man who lingers over his morning newspaper. Oh, John, can you ever forgive me?"

Austin drew in a deep breath to mask his annoyance. "Let's just say that my shoes were sacrificed for a worthy cause. Just out of curiosity, how much money did they earn for your church organ fund?"

She was ashamed to admit that she had practically given them away. "I—sold them for much less than they were worth," she stammered. "You see, the poor man—well, he appeared to have so little—"

"So you sold them for a pittance?"

"Yes. A pittance."

"You haven't touched your coffee. It's getting cold."

"I thought you wouldn't want to give me anything after you discovered what I'd done."

"Well, I won't pretend I'm happy about it, but I can't see that there's anything to be gained by going on about it. Have you had your lunch?"

"No, I haven't even thought about food," Meg admitted. She looked at her watch and realized that the noon hour had come and gone. "Have you had yours?"

"I've been working all morning and just now stopped to take a break. Do you have anything on hand for sandwiches? We could pool our resources and eat out here on the deck. Maybe you'll feel better about all this once you've had something to eat."

"*I'm* not the one who should be made to feel better. *You're* the one who's out a perfectly good pair of shoes. Let me at least bring the lunch, and you can supply the coffee."

"Fair enough. I'm not much good in the kitchen once I get past th coffeepot. Don't go to a lot of trouble, though. Whatever you planned t have for yourself is fine with me."

What she had planned to have was a peanut butter sandwich, but sh couldn't very well admit that. "I'll go downstairs and see what I can find, she said and hurried down the wooden staircase.

Her heart sank when she looked in her cupboard. Not in her wild est dreams had she imagined that she would be "entertaining" durin her "basement days." She pulled a can of corned beef from the shelf an opened it by twisting its key. To this, she added a bit of chopped onion, dollop of sweet pickle relish, and some mayonnaise. She spread her sand wiches on rye bread, added lettuce, wrapped them in plastic, and place them on a big aluminum tray.

From her refrigerator, she retrieved the two eggs that she had hard boiled this morning, intending to have them for her supper tonight. Sh sliced them in half and deviled them. She cut two carrots into matchstick slices. In the bottom drawer of her refrigerator, she discovered a package o juicy, red grapes, which she washed and added to her tray, and at last sh was ready to go upstairs, bearing her "peace offering."

Meg had some difficulty balancing her tray as she negotiated the stone steps up the hillside. When she got to the back door, she was surprised to see the big gray cat sprawled in the same spot he seemed to have chosen as his own personal domain.

John heard her coming and opened the kitchen door for her. His eyes swept over her tray. "I thought we decided to keep this simple."

"It *is* simple," she said. "Anyway, this is the least I could do after I—"

He covered her lips with his fingertips. "Let's don't start on that again. I'd rather talk about something pleasant." He took the tray from her and carried it through the house to the front deck, and Meg followed.

The glass-topped wicker table was covered with a small linen cloth and set with two plates and matching cups and saucers. Austin poured the coffee and helped himself to a sandwich.

A squirrel scampered along a tree limb that brought him within jumping distance, and he landed in the middle of the deck to beg for his lunch. Austin obliged by throwing him a few crumbs.

For several moments, they ate in silence, watching the squirrel snatch up every stray morsel that fell to the floor. Austin noticed that the color had returned to Meg's cheeks, and she was beginning to look more relaxed.

"Tell me something about yourself," he coaxed, thinking of his unfinished manuscript. Perhaps he could pick up on something in Meg's personality to add to the characterization of his protagonist.

"There's not a lot to tell," she began. "In New York, I was a guidance counselor for a girls' boarding school, but I felt ready for a change."

"I'd say you made *quite* a change! Sandy Goodman told me that you teach at a primitive mountain school for most of the year, and only work in the real estate office during the summer. A little country school is certainly a long step from a New York girls' school. What prompted such a big decision?"

Meg began by telling him of the happy years she had spent in the house with her grandmother and of the closeness of their relationship. Then she talked of her work in New York and the shallowness of it all, a thing that she had never discussed with anyone before. She had not planned to tell him of her desire to find a more meaningful path for her life, because these were feelings she had never been able to verbalize even to herself, much less to a virtual stranger. But here in the cool quietness of midday, surrounded by the silent, majestic mountains, her life seemed to unfold like the pages of a book.

As Meg continued to relate her life and her goals, Austin drank in every word. Of all the women he had known in his life, he had never before encountered anyone like Meg—not even close! His fictional character that she had inspired could never measure up to this woman's charm and inner beauty. As her personality unfolded like the petals of a lovely flower, he abandoned his initial resolve to avoid social contacts. He suddenly had a compelling desire to know more about Meg Donnelly before summer's end.

Meg had begun to talk to him about some of her school problems—Bud McLendon, in particular—when she realized that she had been talking constantly for the last twenty minutes. "Oh, dear," she said, hastily rising to her feet. "I don't know what came over me to go on like that!"

"I'm sorry you stopped," he said. "Please sit down and tell me more."

"No, I really must be going. I have to run into town and get my groceries, and maybe I'll be lucky enough to run into the man who has your shoes. I'm certainly going to look for him." She bent to pick up the tray, and suddenly she remembered something else. "John, I'm embarrassed to tell you this, but I do have a pair of shoes in the car. They belonged to Jim, Sandy's husband. I—that is—Sandy thought they might do for you in a pinch. I'll run out and get them."

She was gone for only a few minutes before she returned with Jim Goodman's brown shoes in her hands. "I'm not sure they're the right size, but if you could use them temporarily. . ."

He reached down and took the shoes from her hands. He held them up and looked at them, and could not restrain a chuckle. "Well," he said, holding aloft the shoes that were at least a full size too small for him, "you said they might do in a *pinch*, and I think that's exactly what they would do if I tried to wear them, but I appreciate the thought."

He handed them back to her, and she held them awkwardly, one in each hand. "I know they aren't as nice as yours were, but, well. . ." At a loss for further words, Meg set the shoes on the porch swing and bent down again to pick up her tray.

"Please don't bother with that. I'll clean this up and return your tray later. Thank you for a great lunch. I don't know when I've enjoyed anything so much," he said sincerely.

Meg flashed him a smile before she started down the steep wooden steps. Going through his house was the shortest route to her basement door, but she had already troubled him enough. When she reached the ground level, she rounded the corner of her house and entered her lower-level apartment.

The more she thought about her actions today, the more she was embarrassed by them. First, she had committed the unthinkable by selling John's best shoes, and then she had compounded her error by boring him with details of her life, things that she usually did not share with even her closest friends. And leaving Jim Goodman's shoes on the porch swing for him! Why, he must think her a complete idiot! For some unfathomable reason, his opinion of her was beginning to matter a great deal to Meg.

Chapter 12

Steeple bells sounded through the trees and echoed across the hills, reminding all who paused to listen that this was the day set aside for worship. Responding to their call, Meg pulled on a skirt and blouse, gulped down a cup of instant coffee, and hurried out the door.

She liked to arrive at Sunday school early enough to greet the first children as they arrived in her primary classroom. She knew each one by name because, although they had been too young for her fifth- through eighth-grade schoolroom, they were all pupils at Mountain View Community School.

"Good morning, Miz Donnelly!" One by one, they called to her, and each received a personal greeting in return.

"How d'ya like my new dress?" Molly Akins asked. She twirled around to show the billowing fullness of her skirt. "Mama bought it for me at the *bazaard* sale yesterday!"

"It's lovely," Meg assured her, struggling to conceal her amusement.

"My mama went, too!" Joe-Tom declared. "I got a new baseball cap, and it's got the Atlanta Braves on it. I wanted to wear it today, but Mama wouldn't let me."

Meg acknowledged their comments and put them to work looking up Bible references for their lesson.

"Can I read this one when we get in the circle, Miz Donnelly?"

"We'll see, Susan. Take these strips of paper to mark the verses after you find them."

Meg took crayons and some construction paper from the cupboard and put them on the table for the artwork that would follow her story. She laid out the Sunday school quarterlies and a box of small scissors. When everything was in place and all the children had arrived, Meg drew them around her in a circle and proceeded with the lesson.

She loved working with this group of boys and girls. They were so enthusiastic and inquisitive. The hour always ended before they were ready to leave. Just before they were dismissed, she led them in a closing prayer, allowing each child an opportunity to participate.

"Work on your memory verses for next week," she instructed them.

"Hurry, now. Go and find your parents so you won't be late for church."

As she watched them leave the room, she called good-bye to each one by name, and she reminded them all to come back next Sunday.

After the last child left, Meg pushed the chairs back into place. She picked up scraps of paper from the floor, returned the crayons and scissors to their boxes, and put everything in its proper place. Then she used a wet rag to wash dried paste from the scarred wooden table.

She would be late for church again, just as she was nearly every week, but the small inconveniences of teaching Sunday school were generously rewarded each time she looked into the faces of her precious children.

As she rounded the corner of the church, she could already hear the strains of the first hymn: "Savior, like a shepherd lead us; much we need thy tender care. . . ."

Standing just inside the door, Meg let her eyes wander over the congregation. Standing beside Jim in the second row, Sandy shared his hymnal and fairly beamed with happiness. Beth and her two young friends were there, too, and Meg wondered if Sandy realized how blessed she was to have such a fine, loving family. Meg herself had never been part of such a unit, and watching the Goodmans brought a tender yearning to her heart, a longing that someday she too might know that kind of familial joy.

The small church was nearly filled to capacity. Her eyes scanned the pews for a seat, but stopped short and rested on a familiar blond head only one row from the back. *John Austin!* He was the last person she had expected to run into in church today. But that was unfair! Why was she surprised to see him here, and where else would he be on Sunday morning? Just because he had never discussed his faith with her, she had no right to assume that he had none. Something now about the way he stood with his hymnal in his hands, booming out the words in a rich bass voice, brought a surge of warmth to Meg's heart.

His eyes met hers and he smiled, but he did not stop singing. He was quite handsome, Meg decided as she joined in the familiar refrain and found a seat across the aisle from him.

At the end of the hymn, the congregation took their seats, and the pastor made the morning announcements. "We welcome all who worship with us today," he said. "We'd like to recognize our first-time visitors, so if you're here for the first time, would you please raise your hand, and our usher will give you a card to fill out. We won't embarrass you by asking you to stand, but we want to identify and welcome you at the close of the service."

Meg saw two hands go up next to Beth, and she stole a glance out of the corner of her eye to see if John's hand was raised as well. To her surprise, he sat with his arms folded. She had never thought of him as a shy person, but for some reason, he declined to identify himself as a first-time visitor.

Besides Beth's two friends, only one other visitor held his palm in the air to be recognized. The man sat directly in front of Meg.

The usher moved down the aisle and distributed the cards, and Meg strained to get a better look at the man in front of her with his hand in the air. It looked like—but of course, it could not be! Still, he was tall enough, but from the back it was difficult to tell. He did not wear overalls today. His stiffly starched, blue cotton shirt was faded from countless washings, and his dark hair curled down around the edge of his frayed collar. If she could just get a peek at his shoes! She leaned forward, but she could not see over his shoulders.

Meg tried to focus her attention on the service, but she found it difficult to concentrate on Pastor Blake's sermon. Was it mere coincidence that he had chosen Matthew 25:38 as his text? " 'When saw we thee a stranger, and took thee in? or naked, and clothed thee?' " Her eyes kept involuntarily returning to the back of the stranger's head, and her mind pictured his feet in fine leather shoes. If only she could be sure.

At the close of the service, Meg was determined to be the first person out of the church, and if her hunch was correct, to right the terrible wrong she had committed the day before. But her path was blocked by an elderly lady who had slipped in beside her during the service. The woman stood staunchly at the end of the pew, visiting with one of her friends.

"Excuse me, Mrs. Bettinger," Meg said politely.

The woman turned and gave Meg a sweet smile. "Good morning, my dear. And what is your name?"

"I'm Meg Donnelly. I—"

"Oh, yes, of course! The schoolteacher! How are you, my dear?"

"Fine, thank you. I'm sorry, Mrs. Bettinger, but I'm in a bit of a hurry, so if you'll excuse me. . ."

"You young people are always in a hurry. Well, don't let me stand in your way." Mrs. Bettinger moved into the aisle and allowed Meg to squeeze by.

Meg reached the church lawn in time to see the tall stranger hurrying down the road, and yes, he was wearing a beautiful pair of black leather shoes!

"Sir, wait!" Meg sprinted across the lawn, but before she reached the road, she was stopped by the firm pressure of a hand on her right arm. "Hold on, Meg. It's all right. Let him go."

"Oh, John! But don't you see? That's the man I've been looking for;

the one who bought your shoes. Let go of my arm, and I'll try to catch up with him and explain what happened."

"Please don't. I saw him in church. I recognized my shoes, and my first impulse was the same as yours. But did you see the look of pride on that man's face? Meg, he was in this church for the very first time, and I'd like to think that those shoes had something to do with bringing him here."

"I could offer to buy him another pair," Meg offered weakly.

"But that wouldn't be the same. Don't you see that?"

"And you're willing to just let him have your shoes?"

Austin grinned. "I must admit that if the choice had been mine, I'd have donated a different pair, but it's too late for that now. He bought the shoes, they're his, and that's the end of it." He led her back toward the people who were congregating sociably in front of the church.

Noticing that he walked with a strange hobble, Meg looked down at John's feet and giggled in spite of herself. His long feet which she estimated to be about a size twelve were squeezed into Jim Goodman's size eleven brown shoes. She covered her mouth with her hand. "I'm sorry, John. It's not a bit funny, but—"

She was relieved to see that he was smiling. "No, today it is not funny, but this is the kind of thing that we'll both be able to laugh about a year from now."

Absorbing his words, Meg wondered how she had found him so irritating when they had first met. He was really a very kind and generous man.

"Meg! John!" Sandy waved them over. "I want you to meet my daughter's friends, and John, you haven't even met Beth." Her introductions were followed by a spate of handshaking before she said, "Please come down to our house for dinner. We're eating picnic-style in the backyard, and I've cooked enough to feed an army."

"Oh, Sandy, I couldn't," Meg protested. "You have such a crowd already."

"Some other time, perhaps," Austin said. He noticed the way Beth was studying him, and it made him decidedly uneasy. A college kid would be just the type who might recognize him from a photograph on one of his book jackets. To have his identity revealed now, just when he was beginning to recuperate from a bad case of writer's block, could prove disastrous to his work. He was starting to make real progress on his novel now, and once he was finished, he would be only too glad to sign books, give speeches, or do whatever his readers desired. But right now, he needed a little more time to call his own, to be just plain John Austin, a mountain recluse. He turned his face aside and tried to give the impression that he was looking for someone.

"You have to eat dinner somewhere," Jim reasoned. "You might as well come on over to our house. Otherwise, I'll be eating leftovers for the rest of the week."

"All right," Meg said at last. "Count me in. How about you, John?"

"I wish I could," he said, keeping his chin lowered and avoiding Beth's eyes. "I do appreciate the invitation, but I have to get back to the house. I–I'm expecting a call. Another time, perhaps. But thanks!" He turned toward his car and strode across the grass.

Meg, noting his uncharacteristically awkward gait, allowed her eyes to focus on his feet—feet that were squeezed into Jim Goodman's cast-off shoes. No wonder he limped as though his feet hurt! And she had dared to make a joke of it!

"Who is that guy?" Beth asked. "I've seen him somewhere before."

"I don't think so, Beth. He's not from around here," Sandy replied. "He's the man I told you about, the one who's renting Meg's house for the summer."

"I guess I was wrong, then." Turning to her girlfriends, she said with a grin, "Maybe I was just *wishing* I knew him. He sure is good-looking, isn't he?"

"Down, girl," her mother chided. "He's too old for you! But I do wish he had accepted our invitation for dinner. He is quite charming."

Meg didn't comment as she tried not to let her disappointment show. John probably wanted to hurry home to talk to that Ramona person again.

Meg caught herself and tried to retract her thoughts. She had never been afflicted with jealousy in the past, and she didn't intend to start now. She had to get a grip on herself before she let her emotions spiral out of control. Since John Austin was obviously involved with someone already, growing fond of him could only lead to disappointment and even possible heartbreak.

Meg reminded herself that their relationship was strictly a business deal, anyway. Both of them had made that very clear in the beginning, and from here on out, she would make sure it stayed that way.

Chapter 13

During the next few weeks, Meg gradually adjusted to her new routine. Yet although her days were busy, there was a terrible *sameness* about them. She did not dislike her work in the real estate office, and certainly her fellow workers went out of their way to make her work pleasant. But at the close of each day, she returned to her musty little apartment squeezed into the earth beneath the home she loved and longed to nest in, and the gray walls cloaked her in loneliness.

She had received no more threatening messages, and the shattered windowpane had been replaced. She had almost managed to put Bud McLendon out of her mind. She felt certain that he was either directly or indirectly responsible for her broken window, but in all probability, he had been on one of his drunken sprees and did not even remember what he had done.

Each day when she left the office, she drove to the grocery store or to the park or the library, delaying the return to her apartment until dusk. This schedule allowed her to slip downstairs in the half-light of evening and avoid a face-to-face encounter with John Austin. She had not weakened her resolve to keep their relationship on a business-only basis, and steering clear of him seemed to be the easiest way to insure that resolve.

But there were several things about her tenant that still irked her. For one thing, that big, gray cat continued to sleep on the mat in front of his kitchen door. John *must* be feeding him, even though she had expressly asked him not to. The cat was much too fat to be starving.

And his early-morning telephone calls were a regular event. John always answered them after the second ring, but Meg still found them disturbing. Of course, she had to get up anyway, so she was never quite sure why she found the calls so annoying. She wondered what Ramona looked like and then wondered why she cared.

How happy she would be when fall came again, when she would leave the real estate office behind and return to the challenge of a new group of students. Best of all, she would be living upstairs in her own home, sleeping in her own bed, cooking and baking in her kitchen, and relaxing on her comfortable deck. And every time the telephone rang, the call would be for *her*. Only then would she be able to put all thoughts of John Austin out of her mind forever. And that was what she fully intended to do.

The only time she saw John was on Sunday mornings in church, where he always occupied his same seat near the back door and left as soon as the service ended. Except for a passing "hello," she had not talked with him since that Sunday over three weeks ago when he had declined Sandy's invitation for dinner.

But if Meg thought she was slipping unnoticed into her apartment each evening, she was wrong. Austin stationed himself by the window and watched until her car's headlights rounded the curve and beamed their way up the mountain road. His eyes followed her as she parked her car, crossed the yard, descended the stone steps, and disappeared from his view.

He did not try to deny that he found his landlady extremely attractive. And her attraction ran much deeper than physical beauty, although she possessed more than an ample share of that. But much more significant was an indefinable inner charm that drew Austin's attention and held it like a magnet, refusing to let go. Even in the short time he had known her, he recognized something unique and special about her.

Austin was torn between his desire to give undivided attention to his work and this persistent invasion of his thoughts by one Meg Donnelly. She was driving him crazy! He had relapsed into a severe case of chronic writer's block, and his computer had now lain silent for almost three weeks.

The worst of it was that he saw no way out of his dilemma. Meg had certainly made it crystal clear that she had no personal interest in him, and lately she even seemed to be taking great pains to avoid him. He had begun to think that he should just pack up and go back home to Florida where he belonged.

Yet somehow he felt strangely responsible for her safety. By hurling that threatening message through her glass window, someone had declared war on Meg, and Austin had no illusion that the action was a forgotten, onetime offense. Whoever threw that brick nurtured a terrible grievance, and that—coupled with a subpar mentality—could be deadly.

Living alone in this house, Meg would be extremely vulnerable. Yet she moved in and out with apparent abandon, throwing caution to the wind. Didn't she realize the potential danger of her situation?

Bud McLendon, if in fact he was the culprit, would not lie dormant forever. Austin predicted that he would soon strike again, and when he did, Austin wanted to be on hand to help nail him.

Tonight when Meg parked her car, Austin watched her unload several bags of groceries and struggle to carry them across the yard. Seizing the opportunity, he hurried down the back porch steps to meet her. "Looks like you could use a little help here!"

Meg beamed a grateful smile and allowed him to relieve her of the heaviest bags. Together they carried them down the slope to her door. "Just leave them here by the door," she told him, not wanting him to see inside her sparse living quarters.

He did as he was told and set the bags on the ground. He lingered for just a moment, wondering if she might invite him in. The top of her head just met his chin, and he drew in the fragrance of her windblown hair. Unlike women who wore heavy perfumes, Meg diffused an air as fresh as spring itself, and Austin was reluctant to relinquish it. "I—do you have a moment? I'm afraid I have a confession to make."

"A confession?"

"Well, sort of. But why don't you put your groceries away first and then come upstairs for a cup of coffee? I'll ply you with drink before I unburden my soul."

"Fair enough," she responded, trying to conceal the curiosity betrayed in her voice. "I'll only be a minute."

Austin scaled the hill in record time and tried to bring a semblance of order to his cluttered kitchen. He piled two days' accumulation of dirty dishes into the dishwasher and swept some of the crumbs from the floor.

He was just beginning to start the coffee when she called through the door, "Sorry it took so long. I had to put all my food away."

Austin noticed that she had changed her tailored office clothes for a soft voile dress that accented her femininity. The dainty floral print was sprigged with violets and tiny leaves that matched the mossy green of her eyes. Her hair had been brushed to a glossy sheen and reminded him of cinnamon toast. The sight of her in the doorway almost took his breath away, and he stood for a moment, just looking at her.

"Now, what is this about a confession?" Meg asked.

"Oh, that." He pulled two coffee mugs from the cabinet. "Well, it's about that poor, old cat!"

"Yes, I've noticed that he's still here. I thought we had come to an agreement about that."

"Well, that's where the confession comes in. You see, I didn't feed him at first, just as you requested. I was hoping he would return to his owner. I even carried him out to the road a couple of times to try to give him the message. But just like a boomerang, he always returned to the same spot. Every time I'd think I was rid of him, I'd turn around and find him sleeping on the mat again. When he wasn't sleeping, he was howling for food. I'm afraid I'm a soft touch when it comes to hungry animals. Finally, I couldn't stand his pitiful cries any longer, and I gave him a bowl of milk. But I did use a plastic bowl," he hastened to explain.

Meg could not decide whether to laugh or scream. She too had a soft spot when it came to animals, and under the circumstances, she knew that she would have done the same thing. "So now, what is the next step?"

Austin looked at her with sheepish eyes. "You haven't heard it all yet. There's more."

"Go ahead. I'm listening." Meg tried to make her voice sound severe, straining to keep the corners of her mouth from turning up in a smile.

"When I went to the grocery store, I bought a bag of cat food, and I've been feeding him on a regular basis ever since. Meg, I'm sorry, but I just couldn't let the poor creature starve to death on our doorstep."

By now, Meg could contain her amusement no longer. Her laughter floated in the air like a flurry of pastel confetti. "It looks like we've got us a cat!"

Austin's relief was evident. He had steeled himself for a reprimand. "I guess we'd better give him a name. What do you suggest?"

"Hmm. How about Boomer, short for Boomerang?"

"Sounds appropriate. But I think he deserves something more aristocratic."

"*Aristocratic!* You've got to be kidding! Why, that arrogant trespasser is nothing but a commoner; pure *bourgeois*! I say he gets an ordinary name, like Tom, Dick, or Harry."

"All right, then. Harry it shall be, at least until his rightful owner appears and tells us otherwise." Then he added softly, "At least we've finally agreed on something!"

"I think the coffee's ready," she observed, deliberately changing the subject. "It smells wonderful!"

Austin filled their mugs with the steaming brew. "Let's sit on the deck. It's especially nice out there after the sun goes down."

She followed him through the house and out the front door onto the familiar redwood deck. Sitting in the wicker chairs, they sipped coffee in silence for several minutes. The birds had ceased their singing and the squirrels had returned to their homes in the trees. Only the steady ripple of the brook broke the hush of the starry night.

Meg remembered her resolve to see less of John Austin, but while her mind screamed *less,* her heart kept whispering *more*! Listening to the voice of her heart could be dangerous, but in spite of all her good intentions,

Meg could no longer deny her attraction to him.

"Tell me something, Meg." His voice broke into her thoughts. "I'm grateful to find such a perfect place to spend my summer, but I just can't imagine why you would allow your home to be rented by a stranger. It's obvious that you love this place, and living downstairs must be a terrible inconvenience."

"It's strictly a matter of economics," she explained honestly. "My bills were mounting up faster than I could handle without digging into my savings account. This just seemed to be the only solution."

"You—"

Austin's sentence was interrupted by the ring of the telephone. "Excuse me," he said, rising to answer it. "I'll be right back." He went inside and was gone for only a few minutes when he reappeared on the deck. "It's for you."

Meg wondered who would be calling her tonight. She left him on the deck and moved into the living room. Holding the receiver to her ear, she said, "Hello?"

"Who was that man who answered your telephone?"

"Hal? I thought you were skimming over the ocean on your cruise ship by now."

"I leave early tomorrow morning. I was calling to tell you 'good-bye.' Meg, who was that guy who answered your phone?"

His tone angered Meg, and although she had a perfectly logical answer to his question, she saw no reason to give him one. "Hal, it was very nice of you to call. I hope you have a lovely trip."

"Look here, Meg, I'm sorry if I sounded abrupt. I only want to make sure you're all right."

"I'm fine, Hal. Send me postcards and tell me all the fun things you're doing, and call me when you get back. Be sure to take lots of pictures!"

"And you aren't going to answer my question, are you?"

"No, Hal. I'm not."

"Just tell me this, Meg. Are you seeing someone? What's going on with you?"

Meg was suddenly aware that John had come into the house and was standing behind her. Was he eavesdropping on her conversation? She looked at him with arched eyebrows that spoke a silent question mark.

"Is everything all right?" John asked. He seemed genuinely concerned.

"Yes, everything is fine."

"What? What's fine?" Hal demanded.

"No, Hal, I was talking to someone else. Look, I really have to hang up now, but bon voyage, and don't forget to write." Without waiting for his reply, Meg replaced the receiver in its cradle.

"I'm sorry," Austin apologized. "I didn't mean to disrupt your conversation. I just wanted to make sure that you were not being threatened again."

"No, that was just a call from a friend in New York."

"A special friend?" Austin felt a terrible need to know.

"Yes, I guess you could call him that," Meg said. "We've been friends for a long time. I–I'm very fond of him." Turning her face toward the deck, she said, "I suppose our coffee is cold by now. Anyway, I should be going."

Austin was stung with disappointment. On the deck, he had begun to feel that their conversation might be leading to a closer bond between them, but now the spell had been broken. "Can we do this again?" He followed her through the house to the kitchen.

"I hope so." Meg opened the back door and stepped carefully over the cat. "Good night."

"Meow!"

"The lady wasn't talking to you, Harry. She was talking to me. Good night, Meg." Austin stood on the porch until she disappeared down the slope and he heard the sound of her key in her door.

"Harry, my friend," he said, reaching down to stroke the cat's sleek coat, "there goes one classy lady, but I get the distinct impression she'd like to give both of us the boot."

"Meow!"

Chapter 14

On Saturday morning, Meg woke to the overhead whining of John's printer. It had been strangely silent for several weeks now, and she had begun to think that his work, whatever that might be, had been completed. Oddly, the noise that she had found so irritating in the past did not seem to disturb her today. Instead, it served to project on her mind the image of John Austin bent over his computer, a lock of his sandy hair falling carelessly over his forehead, his piercing brown eyes intent upon his work.

She simply had to get over this juvenile infatuation that seemed to be consuming her lately. In the first place, there was no future in it for her. In only a few weeks, John Austin would be leaving North Carolina and vanishing from her life forever. She would probably never see him again. And in the second place, she knew very little about him; certainly not enough to consider a romantic relationship with him, even if he were not already involved with someone else. And finally, as she had explained so many times to Hal, she was not in the market for romance at this stage of her life. She had set some lofty goals for herself, and until she achieved at least some of them, she did not want to dilute her efforts by filling her mind with romance.

Today was her first free Saturday since school ended. Last Saturday she had spent the day working with the library committee, getting ready for the dedication of their new bookmobile. The committee had honored her by choosing her as head speaker for that event. On weekends prior to that, she had volunteered her time to bake sales, rummage sales, and other church and community activities. But today was completely her own!

Meg rolled out of her bed and folded it into a couch. She hurried through breakfast to give herself an early start on the day. Today she planned to hike up the mountain to see Sophie Caruthers, an elderly widow who lived a steep mile away. Meg loved to visit the dear old lady and made a point of doing so on a regular basis. But what with the move and all her other obligations, she had not seen Sophie since the beginning of summer.

Sophie did not get out of her house often. A semi-invalid, she depended on the services of a rural nurse who visited her each week, bringing a supply of groceries and medicine. Frequent visits by Meg and some other women of the church were a lifeline for the shut-in, bringing her bits of local news and helping her with simple household chores.

Meg dressed in a pair of denim shorts and a cotton shirt. She chose her sturdiest shoes and added an old straw hat to shield her face from the sun.

She took a small basket from her cupboard shelf. Blackberries were abundant at this time of the year, and she would pick some along the way to take to Sophie. Perhaps she would even bake her a pie.

Meg stepped outside into the fresh morning air and inhaled the fragrance of summer. Wildflowers dotted the surrounding hills and filled the air with their rich perfume.

She kept a supply of hiking sticks in an earthenware crock beside her back door. She chose a sturdy one to help her climb the mountain path. Meg loved trekking through the woods in summer. The ground was covered with dead leaves of winter, and overhead, a lacy green canopy sheltered her from the heat of the sun. Beneath the leaves and in the bushes, unseen creatures scurried out of her way as Meg pushed herself up the incline.

Just as she had suspected, blackberries grew in profusion, plump, juicy ones that weighed down the limbs of their thorny bushes. Her basket was full in no time, in spite of the prickly barbs and the many berries that made a detour to her mouth. Her fingertips were stained a dark purple, and she suspected that her lips bore the same telltale color. Even her shirt was smudged with streaks of the nectar whose sweet taste lingered on her tongue. Sophie was sure to be pleased with them.

The hard climb caused Meg to stop several times along the way, but at last the path turned sharply, and she knew that she was almost there. Her breath was coming rapidly and her forehead was dotted with beads of perspiration. A drink of cold water from Sophie's pump would taste so good!

As she approached the small log cabin, Meg was surprised to hear a loud, pounding noise. She drew into the clearing and discovered its source. Three workmen were sitting on top of Sophie's roof, their busy hammers creating a steady rhythm that echoed through the trees.

Intent on their work, the men did not appear to see Meg as she walked across the clearing and up to the front door. "Sophie?" She pounded on the door, but with so much hammering, she was sure that Sophie could not hear her knock. She eased the door open a crack and stuck her head inside. "Sophie, it's only me—Meg. I've brought you some berries."

"Land sakes, child, come in here. You're a sight for sore eyes!" Sophie was seated in a cherry rocker, her knees covered with a light cotton afghan. A big grin sliced her wrinkled face. "Come on in here, honey. I'm just mighty glad to see you."

"And I'm glad to see you, too, Sophie. How have you been?"

"I'm just fine, honey, thanks to the good Lord who sends me friends like you and all the others. Did you see what the fellers are doing to my roof?"

"I saw some men working on it. Tell me what's going on."

"Well, you know that nurse that comes to see me every Wednesday? Well, she noticed how bad my roof was leaking. It's been doing that for a long time, but I don't pay it no mind, because I've got plenty of pots to set around and catch the water, but she put up a big fuss and said I had to have it fixed. Well, she sent a man out here to look at it, and when he told me how much it was going to cost, I just laughed at him. I figured that was the end of it, but the preacher, he just happened to be here that day, and next thing I knew, he had these fellers up here working on it for me. This is the third day they've come, but I think they plan to finish today. I told them I'd pay them off, a little each month, but they wouldn't hear tell of it. Said they were just doing the Lord's work."

"That's wonderful, Sophie. I know they're happy to be able to help you."

"Well, I wished there was some way I could do something for them. It would sure make me feel a whole lot better about it."

"I'll tell you what, Sophie! Why don't I fix us all something for lunch? I see that your garden is in pretty good shape. I could make a big pot of vegetable soup and some biscuits and a blackberry pie, and we could invite them to come in and eat with us."

Sophie's eyes sparkled with delight, and she clapped her hands. "Land sakes, Meg, what a wonderful idea! Why, I'd love a bowl of fresh vegetable soup myself, and those blackberries you brought will make a grand pie!"

Meg found everything she needed for soup in the garden. She picked pole beans, okra, tomatoes, and corn, and she dug up sweet potatoes and beets and carrots. Working along the rows of the well-tended patch, she was sure that some of the kind people from the church had lent their hands to cultivate it.

Overhead, she could hear the hammers' relentless pounding. How blessed Sophie was to have such a fine, loving group of Christian friends.

Meg washed and pared the vegetables and soon had a big kettle of soup bubbling on the stove. She collected all the peelings in a dishpan, to add to Sophie's compost pile in the backyard later. She put a deep-dish blackberry pie in the oven to bake while she rolled out dough for buttermilk biscuits. The enticing aroma filled the small cabin and drifted out the windows to mingle with the mountain air.

While lunch cooked, Meg sat beside Sophie and read aloud a few passages from the Bible. Failing eyesight made reading difficult for the aging woman, and she delighted in Meg's clear, young voice delivering the words from her favorite book. Then Meg laid the Bible aside and began to tell her all the things that had recently happened around the little area known as Mountain View. She told Sophie about her job at the real estate office in Shady Valley and how Sandy had helped her get it. She gave her an updated report on the progress of the library's new bookmobile. "Soon they'll be driving right out here to Mountain View every week, and all our folks will be able to check out books and magazines to read." Meg told her about the growing church organ fund, and the various moneymaking projects she and others were working on. "We hope to have enough money to buy a secondhand organ before Christmas. It would add so much to the children's annual pageant." Meg even told her about her new tenant and the adjustments she had been forced to make in her lifestyle to accommodate him.

Sophie loved companionship, and she hung onto Meg's words as though they were cookie crumbs given to a starving child. The rural nurse brought her newspapers each week and brought her up to date on state and national events, but only a "local" could fill her in on the kind of neighborhood news she craved. "Tell me some more about that man you've got living in your house, honey. Is he married?"

Meg colored. "No, I don't believe that he is." She rose from her chair. "I think our soup should be just about ready, Sophie. I'd better pop the biscuits in the oven and set the table. How many workers do you have up there on your roof?"

"I think there's three," Sophie said. "And you and me, that makes five."

Meg removed her pie from the oven and set it on the back of the stove. She tasted the soup and added an extra pinch of salt.

The kitchen table was covered with red checkered oilcloth. Meg wiped it clean and set five places. She was just about to call the men inside for lunch when the three of them lumbered through the front door.

"We don't know what you're cooking in here, Sophie, but whatever it is, we want some of it."

Meg did not recognize the first two men who came in, but as the third man stepped through the door, she caught her breath. "John Austin! What are you doing here?"

"Hello, Meg. To answer your question, I'm helping repair this nice lady's roof. What are you doing here?"

Meg was momentarily flustered. "Uh, I just came up to visit Sophie, and right now, I'm putting lunch on the table. I didn't expect to find you here. Come sit down," she urged, using a wide sweep of her hand to include all three men in her invitation. She wondered how John had come to know Sophie, but she did not ask.

"We'll have to wash up first."

After the men had filed out to the pump, Meg turned to Sophie. "That last man, John Austin, he's the man I told you about, the one I'm renting my house to this summer. How did he become involved in this project?"

"Why, I don't know, honey. The preacher arranged everything. It's been a different bunch to come each day except for that one you're talking about. He's been here every day." Even with failing eyesight, Sophie did not miss Meg's rising color. "He's kinda handsome, isn't he?"

"I–I hadn't noticed. I'd better make some tea. I expect those men will all be thirsty." Meg turned her back to Sophie and returned to the stove. Behind her, she could hear Sophie chuckling to herself.

"Hand me my cane, honey. It takes me a spell to get to the table, so I'd best get started."

Meg did as she was told and then folded Sophie's afghan and laid it across the back of the rocking chair. She watched Sophie struggle to the table, but knowing how the old woman valued her independence, Meg did not try to assist her.

When the men returned and took their places around the table, Sophie said a blessing: "Lord, we sure do thank You for this good food. You sent rain and sunshine to grow these fine vegetables, and You sent helping hands to prepare them. And Lord, I just want to thank You for all these people that have come up here to help me out. Bless them one and all, and bless this food we are about to eat, and make us thankful. In Jesus' name we pray. Amen." A chorus of amens echoed around the table.

Meg had thought that the big kettle of soup would provide enough leftovers to feed Sophie for the entire week, but the hearty appetites of hardworking men almost cleaned the pot. Meg received lavish compliments on her blackberry pie. "The best I ever tasted," Sophie declared, and no one disagreed.

After lunch, the men returned to their work, and Meg cleaned up Sophie's kitchen. "I've saved all the vegetable peelings for your compost pile. I'll put them out on the heap before I leave."

Returning to the garden in the backyard, Meg emptied her dishpan, filled with peelings and scraps, on the pile of decomposing garbage that Sophie used as fertilizer.

When she returned to the house, she noticed that Sophie looked tired. "Why don't you lie down for a nap?" she suggested.

"Honey, I can nap anytime. I'd a heap rather visit with you."

"Well, you just make yourself comfortable, Sophie, because it's time for me to leave. I wouldn't want to be caught out on the mountain after dark. I might meet up with a hungry bear."

"Well, stay here for just another minute," Sophie urged. "I think I hear the men coming down from the roof."

Only one of the men came to the door. The other two stayed outside to clean the yard of shingle scraps and fallen debris. "We've finished your roof, ma'am. We don't think you'll have any more leaks, but if you do, just tell Preacher Blake, and he'll get us back up here again."

"Go outside and get the others," Sophie commanded. "I want a word with all of you men before you leave."

When the man left to get his helpers, Meg bent to kiss the wrinkled cheek. "Well, I'll just be running on, Sophie. I'll visit you again soon." She picked up her basket and eased toward the door, but Sophie stopped her.

"Could you leave that basket with me for a spell, Meg? Just set it there on the table. I got a use for it, but I'll see that you get it back soon."

"Of course." Meg eyed her quizzically, but she did as she was requested. "Keep it as long as you have a need for it, Sophie. I have several others." Meg was doubly puzzled, because this proud old woman seldom asked anyone for anything.

As she crossed the yard, she passed the three workmen moving toward the cabin door. "Thanks again for the lunch," one man called, and the other two echoed his gratitude.

"I'm glad you enjoyed it," Meg replied. "Sophie's a dear lady, and it was nice of you fellows to pitch in to help her."

Walking down the mountainside proved to be even harder than climbing up had been. Meg used her hiking stick to keep her feet from sliding along the damp, sloping earth. She had not gone far when she heard hurrying footsteps behind her and, turning, was surprised to see John Austin catching up with her.

"Where are the others?" she asked.

"They're still back there with Sophie. She was worried because you left without your basket." He handed her the basket and tried to explain. "She gave it to me and asked if I thought I could catch up with you. I told her I'd just take it and leave it by your door, but she didn't like that idea. She said you might want to fill it with blackberries on your way home." He looked puzzled. "I didn't quite understand. She asked the other two guys to wait for a few minutes because she wanted to visit with them, but she seemed extremely anxious to hurry me on before you got too far down the mountain."

Austin stepped ahead of her and proceeded down the mountainside in front of her, to block her path in case she should fall.

"Why, that little schemer!" Meg had to laugh. "I know exactly what she's up to."

"Well, tell me, because I don't get it!"

Meg had no intention of telling him that Sophie was an incurable romantic who enjoyed playing the role of matchmaker. She should have realized what was going through Sophie's mind when she saw that mischievous gleam in her eye. To sidestep his question, Meg said, "That's just Sophie. You never can tell what she's—*ooh!*" But before she finished her sentence, Meg's heel slid out from under her, and she would have fallen down the steep incline if Austin had not been there to catch her. Instead, she slid straight into his arms, and he held her securely against his chest.

Meg was shaken. She put her hands on John's shoulders to regain her balance and felt his steady arms around her waist, strong and comforting. For several seconds she stood perfectly still, looking into his piercing brown eyes, feeling his warm breath on her cheek, and suddenly her knees felt like two pieces of wet cardboard. When she swayed slightly, he tightened his hold on her.

"Are you all right?" he asked.

"Yes. Yes, I'm fine," she assured him, pushing herself free of his embrace. She smoothed her shirt and brushed back the lock of hair that had fallen across her face. "You saved me from a bad fall."

"I've had a few close calls myself, going up and down this mountain. It's pretty steep."

"John, how did you get involved in this project? Are you a professional carpenter?"

Austin chuckled. "No, far from it. I don't even put up my own closet shelves at home. But when Pastor Blake asked for some men to help work on Sophie's roof, it seemed that most of the men from the church were already committed to regular jobs during the week. Some of them volunteered to give up one day to help, but my schedule was pretty flexible, so I gave them three."

"That was very kind of you."

"You showed a bit of Christian kindness today yourself, dear lady! Do you go up there to call on Sophie often?"

"Not as often as I should, I guess. She leads a pretty lonely life. She'd rather have company than an ice cream cone!"

"Ice cream cones! I haven't had one since I left Florida in June, and I have a real passion for them! Is there any place around here that sells them?"

"Not here in the Mountain View community, but there's a drive-in in Shady Valley that sells the old-fashioned, hand-dipped kind. Thirty-seven flavors! I'll draw a map for you when we get back to the house."

"I have a much better idea. Let's get cleaned up and ride in town together to get some. Could we maybe have dinner first? What kind of food do they sell at this drive-in?"

Meg's heart skipped a beat. "John Austin, are you asking me out?"

"It sounded that way, didn't it? Yes, I guess I am."

"Then I accept." Meg felt like a giddy teenager being asked to the prom. No invitation that she had received in recent years had excited her as this one did. She barely remembered that on this very day she had rejected any idea of romance, and all of the promises she had made to herself in the light of early morning hours melted away like butter on a warm summer day.

Chapter 15

On Monday morning, Meg sat at her desk at Hanson Real Estate Company and greeted the first clients who walked through the door with a pleasant smile. "Good morning! How can I help you?"

A retired couple who had rented a small mountain cottage for the summer liked the location so much that they were now ready to discuss buying something in the area. Meg introduced them to one of the Hanson agents, and they were promptly whisked away into one of the private cubicles.

Between the busy reception room and the constantly ringing telephones, Meg had little time to think about her weekend until almost noon. But with the first lull of business, her thoughts flipped back to Saturday night and the hours she had spent with John Austin.

The man remained an enigma. In many ways, he seemed to be exactly the kind of man she had always hoped to meet—a kind and thoughtful Christian—yet there was something illusive and strange about him. In spite of her questions, he had never shared with her any of the details of his life in Florida—only that he had suffered from work burnout and needed a complete change. When she tried to press him for more information, he always managed to change the subject with such skillful subtlety that she scarcely realized what had happened until after the fact. No doubt about it, John Austin was a master with words. She guessed that he might even be a lawyer, but why would he not want to tell her that? Why all this secrecy?

Was he hiding from something or someone? It almost seemed that way, because when they went to Shady Valley for supper at the drive-in Saturday night, he had rejected the idea of eating inside, insisting instead on their using the curbside service and eating inside his car. Although this turned out to be a messy business, Meg had to admit she thoroughly enjoyed every morsel. Eating with their fingers, they had consumed baskets of southern-style, batter-dipped fried chicken along with coleslaw and greasy french fries. They had giggled like schoolkids while they ate old-fashioned double dips of chocolate ice cream and licked the sweet, sticky drips that ran down the sides of their cones.

After their appetites were satiated, she had suggested that he might enjoy walking down the main street, stopping on the courthouse lawn to watch "Pickin' on the Square." Every Saturday night, locals gathered with banjos and guitars to stage this lively, foot-stomping exhibition of country music. But John had chosen to park two blocks from the square, rolling the car windows down so that they could sit and listen to the music, away from the crowds.

Later, after they had returned to the house, John had insisted that she come in while he made a fresh pot of coffee, and they sat together on the deck, enjoying the stillness of the moonlit night. The change in his demeanor was obvious, replacing caution and wariness with peaceful repose.

She had felt his eyes focus on her face and wished that she could read his thoughts. Meg could sense a magnetic current between them that electrified her in a way she was powerless to understand. Did John feel it, too? Her head continued to sound warning bells of the possible dangers in becoming involved with a man of whom she knew so little, yet her heart seemed to have a mind of its own, one that was completely oblivious to the warning signals.

"Meg?"

"Oh, I'm sorry, Mr. Hanson. I–I'm afraid I was woolgathering on the job. I won't let that happen again." To say that she was embarrassed would be an understatement.

But her employer was smiling. "We all do that during odd moments, Meg. I'm sure that the ring of your telephone would have reawakened you to your duties. Let me assure you that I have no complaints about the way you're handling this job. In fact, if I hadn't been told of your dedication to the teaching profession, I might try to interest you in a permanent position here."

Meg smiled her gratitude.

Her employer continued. "I was just wondering if you were planning on going to lunch today. It's after twelve already. I'll have someone cover for you while you're away from your desk."

"Thank you, Mr. Hanson. The morning has gone by so fast that I didn't realize it was lunchtime." Meg pulled her leather purse from the bottom drawer and hurried to wash her hands.

By the time Meg arrived at the corner café, Sandy, Lucy, and Gina had already given their orders to the waitress. Meg slid into the booth beside them. "What's the special for today?"

"Country-fried steak and mashed potatoes. That's what we're all having."

"Just make that four," Meg told the waitress, "and I'd like a tall glass of unsweetened iced tea."

While they waited for their food, the four women shared news of their weekend. "My husband wouldn't miss 'Pickin' on the Square' every Saturday night," Gina declared. "Say, Meg, I thought I saw you at the drive-in, sitting in a big, fancy car. Are you holding out on us?"

Meg's cheeks burned. "Not at all," she said defensively. "I did have dinner at the drive-in with a friend, but that isn't earth-shattering news."

"Well, I don't blame you for keeping him on the outside," Gina chided. "A guy that good-looking should be kept a secret as long as possible."

Sandy's interest peaked. "Who took you to the drive-in, Meg? That man who's working with you on the new county bookmobile?"

"No." Meg was happy that the waitress chose that moment to put their plates on the table, and she declined to carry the conversation further. Since Sandy picked up her fork and began to attack her food, Meg assumed that she had forgotten the matter, but that assumption did not last through the afternoon.

As soon as Meg returned to the office, Sandy came to her desk wearing a big, face-splitting grin. "I'll wager a guess that it was John Austin who took you out Saturday night. Am I right?"

"My goodness, Sandy. Why is everyone making such a big thing out of this? It was just a neighborly gesture on his part, not like a date. I expect he's already forgotten the whole thing. Besides, I think he is already involved with someone back in Florida. They seem to talk on the phone a lot."

"But he isn't in Florida now," Sandy reminded her, still maintaining her grin. "He's in North Carolina, and so are you! I've seen the way he looks at you, Meg."

"Get back to your work, Sandy. You've been watching too many movies."

The two women did not have a chance to carry their conversation farther, because the telephone rang and Meg reached to answer it. "Good afternoon. Hanson Realty. How may I direct your call?"

"Miss Donnelly, please."

"Speaking. Who's calling, please?"

"Miss Donnelly, this is Deputy Scarsdale. Sheriff Gallagher asked me to call you."

"Is something wrong?" Meg's heart skipped a beat. She had not heard from the sheriff or his deputy since the night the brick bearing that ugly note had sailed through her kitchen window. She had been so busy since then that she had almost been able to put the incident out of her mind.

She didn't really want any reminders.

"No, nothing's wrong, and I don't want to unduly alarm you. But we thought you should know that Bud McLendon's appeal to regain custody of his son was denied this afternoon. He stormed out of the courtroom and headed straight for the nearest bar. We've seen his behavioral pattern before, Miss Donnelly. His temper mixed with whiskey almost always leads to acts of violence. Of course, even if he does follow his usual pattern, we have no idea where he will direct his rage at this time. He has plenty of enemies. But we do know he's been telling anyone who will listen to him that you are the person responsible for taking away his son. We'll try to keep an eye on him for the next few days, but we think you should use caution. If you go out at night, I'd suggest you have someone else go along with you."

"I've met head-to-head with Bud McLendon before, Deputy. I think he's just a big bully with a bark that's worse than his bite. But I'll use normal caution, and I do appreciate the warning. By the way, how is young Billy?"

"He seems to be doing remarkably well. I talked to his foster mother this afternoon, to give her the same warning I just gave you. She says that Billy seems happy, but he has a pathetic fear of being returned to his father. She and her husband are petitioning the court for permanent custody. They'd like to adopt Billy and take him away from this area."

"And Billy wants that?"

"Very much. He loves his dad, and he worries about him, but he's also afraid of him. He doesn't want to live with him."

"I've been praying for that child, asking God to take care of him. Billy is a good boy, and he deserves a better life than he has known in the past. I'd be so happy to know that he was permanently placed with a family who loved him."

"I've been praying for him, too, Miss Donnelly, along with a lot of other people. I'd say our prayers are being answered."

When Meg hung up the receiver, she paused a few moments to thank God for answered prayer. And she prayed that Billy would find God's plan for his life and follow it.

Deputy Scarsdale's warning flashed across her mind. She would take all normal precautions as she had promised, but she refused to live her life in fear, running and hiding from the likes of Bud McLendon. She had things to do and commitments to fulfill. Some of those obligations involved going out at night, but she had no intention of finding someone to tag along playing nursemaid to her.

Tonight she was scheduled to meet with the bookmobile committee in the library's conference room. Because it didn't make good sense for her to drive all the way home and then back to Shady Valley again, she planned to pick up a sandwich from the drive-in and go straight to her meeting.

The meeting tonight was to set up a filing system to help them keep track of books. The bookmobile itself was so costly that there was no money left in their treasury to purchase new books yet, but the people of Shady Valley and surrounding communities had been extremely generous in donating their used books. Dozens of boxes of books were stacked in the library basement, waiting to be sorted and cataloged.

On Friday evening, the committee would meet again, this time to unpack the boxes of books and stock the bookmobile shelves in readiness for the dedication ceremony next week. After that, the library on wheels would be ready to roll! Meg had worked so hard and waited so long for this dream to become a reality. She could hardly believe that it was actually about to happen!

Chapter 16

The meeting of the bookmobile committee lasted longer than all its members had expected, and excitement ran high. The treasurer had reported a balance that would allow them to purchase all the needed supplies for opening day and still have enough left over to purchase a few new books.

When the meeting was over, Meg walked with two friends to her car in the library parking lot. "Pinch me so I'll know I'm not dreaming! I'm just so elated about all this!" she exclaimed.

"We all are," Cameron Brown agreed. "But you're the one who deserves all the credit, Meg."

"Oh, no. Certainly not."

Alice Robards said, "Cameron's right, Meg. Or at least, if you won't accept all the credit, you surely deserve most of it. The whole idea was yours in the first place, and you've put your heart and soul in this project. You've worked hard on it for months, and we all owe you a vote of thanks."

"Well, please don't waste any of our treasury money on flowers for me," Meg insisted. "The opening of the bookmobile will be reward enough. We've all worked long and hard on this thing, but now at last our labors are going to pay off!"

Standing on the black asphalt of the parking lot, they said their good-byes, and Meg slid into the driver's seat of her blue compact. As she started to back out of her space, she heard a strange, flopping sound, and her car lurched awkwardly.

"What—?" She opened her car door and climbed out to determine her problem. Under the illumination of high incandescent lights, she circled and examined her car. Her heart sank to the pit of her stomach when she saw that she had not one but two flat tires. "Oh, no! I can't believe this!" She raised both hands to her head, as though she expected to awake from this terrible nightmare, but no amount of denial could erase the glaring facts. "Two flat tires, and I have only one spare! What am I going to do?"

Alice Robards was just pulling her car out onto the street when she looked in her rearview mirror and saw Meg's distressing plight. She stopped, made a U-turn, and returned to offer her help.

After pulling up beside Meg, Alice slid out of her car and stood beside her. She shook her head in dismay. "You must have run over some nails or something," she surmised. "It's eerie to have two tires go flat at the same time. I could help you change them, but you probably don't have two spare ones, do you?"

"No, I don't, and I imagine that all the local service stations would be closed by now. I'll have to leave the car here until morning and call a taxi to take me out to Mountain View."

"Indeed you won't! I wouldn't hear of it. Just lock everything up and hop in my little buggy. I'll drive you home."

"Alice, do you know where I live? It's almost fourteen miles from here."

"I know. But what are friends for? Get in. We're wasting time."

Meg retrieved her purse and briefcase from the front seat of her car and locked the doors. The parking lot would remain lighted all night. Her car should be relatively safe here. At least, no one was likely to drive it away with two flat tires!

She climbed into the passenger's side of Alice's car. "Do you need to call your husband to tell him why you'll be getting home so late? It's after ten o'clock already."

"He's in Raleigh at a lumberman's convention. I'm on my own tonight."

"But if he calls and you're not there, won't he be concerned?"

"Quit worrying, Meg. Are you always such a worrywart?" Alice teased good-naturedly. "My Sid would expect me to do just exactly what I am doing—helping a friend in need. In fact, he'd be disappointed in me if I left you stranded out here with no transportation, so just lean back and enjoy the ride." Alice flipped on the radio and strains of country music filled the car, while Meg breathed a silent prayer of thanksgiving for friends like Alice.

There was little traffic on the road at this hour. A light rain had begun to fall, and the steady swish of the wipers seemed to keep time to the music as Alice's car traveled through the dark night.

Sitting silently in the corner of the front seat, Meg visualized the bills she would be forced to face, if not for new tires, at least for road service and repair. Would there be no end to the demands on her bank account? Every time she thought she could see herself moving forward, something like this came along to push her back. She felt as though she were trying to move up a down escalator. "My tires are almost new," she lamented aloud.

"You may have run over some broken glass or picked up some nails. I had that happen to me once when I drove out to one of Sid's construction sites. I drove right over some old boards spread on the ground. Sid said I should have known better, but I didn't even think about the possible consequences until it was too late."

"I suppose you're right, but I don't remember driving over anything like that. "Alice, you'd better start slowing down after you round the next curve. You're coming up on the dirt road that turns up to Mountain View. It's just around the next corner. You're an angel to bring me way out here like this, but I hate the thought of your having to drive back to Shady Valley alone."

"I don't mind. Really, I don't. Sid's gone so much of the time that I've become used to acting as my own chauffeur. I'm just glad I noticed your problem before I drove off and left you stranded in the library parking lot."

The crunch of Alice's tires on dirt and gravel broke the silence of the night as the car climbed up the mountain road. Passing Sandy's house, Meg saw that her lights were out. "My house is just around this next curve," she said, pointing with her forefinger.

"All your lights are on. Do you have company?"

Meg was forced to explain her unusual summer rental agreement. "It's a temporary inconvenience for me, but at least it's helping to solve some of my financial problems."

"I'm sorry. I didn't know." Alice pulled her car into the drive as far as John's bulky car would permit. "I'll wait to make sure you get inside okay. Here, use this plastic bag to cover your hair. Sorry I didn't bring an umbrella."

"Alice, I don't know how to thank you—" Meg began.

"Hush! Run, now, before you get soaked to the skin and catch pneumonia!"

Meg covered her hair with the plastic bag and made a dash for her house. She had to slow down and move carefully as she approached the incline that led to her basement. Edging down the sloping earth, she turned and waved to Alice before she disappeared from view. "Thanks!" she called over her shoulder, and almost slipped on the wet stones as she gingerly stepped down the last few feet to her door.

Seated at her desk the next morning, Meg had time to wonder how much the bill from Archie's Garage was going to deplete her bank account. She had called them early this morning, and Archie himself had promised to have her car ready and delivered to her office before five o'clock. That was a relief! Meg did not have money to waste on taxis, and she hated to impose on her friends. But Archie could well afford to put himself out for her, Meg thought cynically. She had already called him twice this month. Surely she must be one of his best customers!

"Good morning! Hanson Realty. How may I direct your call?" she said into the telephone.

"Miss Donnelly? Deputy Scarsdale here."

"Oh, good morning, sir. I appreciate your calling to check on me, but I'm happy to report that I have had no further—"

"It's about your car, ma'am."

"My car?" *How did the sheriff's department get involved with my car?* "What is this call about, Deputy?" Meg felt an involuntary shiver as she listened for an answer she was not at all sure she wanted to hear.

"Archie down at the garage called us a few minutes ago to file a report on an act of vandalism. Seems like somebody decided to stick a knife in two of your tires last night. What can you tell me about that?"

Meg's head spun dizzily, and she struggled to catch her breath. "I–I never even considered that possibility. I just thought I must have run over some nails or something. Are you sure it was done intentionally? Is there any way to determine who might have done such a thing?"

"I'm afraid not. Last night's rain washed away any possibility of picking up tire tracks, and no one reported seeing any suspicious activity in that area. There's no way we can prove anything, no matter how strongly we suspect—uh—anyone. Have you received any more threatening notes or calls or seen anything that we might use to give us a clue?"

"No, nothing! Last night I attended a meeting in the library that lasted until late in the evening, but the parking lot is well lighted. It's hard to imagine anyone was brazen enough to slash tires under a bright light."

"Not really; not when you consider everything else that has happened recently. Miss Donnelly, I want to caution you again against going out at night alone. I hope we can soon find a way to put an end to all this business, but until we do, please be careful."

"Thank you, Deputy. I guess we both have a pretty good idea who might stoop to such a low, mean trick. I'll keep my eyes open."

As she replaced the receiver on the telephone, Meg realized that her hands were shaking, and a chill swept through her body. She had to get a grip on herself. She lowered her head into her hands and murmured a silent prayer. As anxiety was replaced with composure, she heard the telephone ringing again.

"Good morning! Hanson Realty. How may I direct your call?"

True to his promise, one of Archie's men delivered the car to her at five o'clock, just as she was preparing to lock her desk. He came into the office and stood holding his cap in his hands. Still in his greasy work clothes, he seemed embarrassed as he laid an invoice on her desk. Meg examined the bill and decided that Archie must truly have a heart after all, because the charges were surprisingly reasonable. Meg reached for her purse and wrote the man a check. "Thank you," she said, giving him the check and accepting her keys from his outstretched hand. "I'm glad I didn't have to buy new tires."

"Archie said to tell you he's sorry about what happened to your car. He don't like things like that happenin' in Shady Valley. He always tells everybody that comes into the garage that we're the friendliest town in North Carolina, and when somethin' like this happens, it makes him hoppin' mad."

"Well, you tell Archie that one bad incident isn't going to change my mind about the folks of Shady Valley. As far as I'm concerned, he can still claim bragging rights. Do I need to take you back to the garage?"

"No, ma'am. I got a buddy outside, waitin' to pick me up."

Meg watched him leave the office before she gathered her belongings and went outside to reclaim her car.

On the way out of town, she stopped at the supermarket to pick up a few groceries. With the bookmobile dedication scheduled for Friday, the next few days would be busy ones, and she would not have a lot of time to worry about her meals. She decided to buy an eye-of-round beef roast that would fit in her slow-cooker. With it, she could throw in a few vegetables and have dinner ready when she returned from work in the evening.

She chose a roast big enough to leave leftovers for the entire week. She moved through the produce department, making her selections quickly and tossing them into her grocery cart. Having stayed out so late last night, she was bone tired and eager to get home for a shower and bed. No doubt, the mental strain of the last twenty-four hours was taking a toll on her body, too.

She pushed her cart along the aisle toward the checkout counter and stepped into one of the lines. When the tall man in front of her turned his profile toward her as he paid for his purchases, she drew in her breath sharply. Even with his dark glasses on, there was no mistaking his identity.

John Austin's groceries, she noted, consisted mostly of TV dinners and fresh fruit. *Why*, she wondered, *would anyone wear dark glasses inside the store? Unless. . .*

She did not get to finish her thought because, at that moment, he turned and recognized her. "Well, if it isn't my favorite landlady!"

"Paper or plastic, sir?" the clerk asked before bagging his groceries.

"Plastic. Paper. Whatever." He turned back to Meg as she unloaded the contents of her cart onto the counter. "I'm glad to see you're out and about today. I was worried last night when you were so late getting home, especially when you didn't have your car."

Just the mere sound of his voice had turned her legs to jelly. Meg started to explain what had happened, but then she thought better of it. She did not need to account for her whereabouts to him, or to anyone else, for that matter. "Oh, I'm fine." She smiled, but kept her voice primly polite and impersonal. "But I appreciate your concern," she thought to add.

Austin picked up his bags of groceries and stood as though he had more to say.

Meg concentrated on the items from her cart as the clerk passed them over the scanner. She was well aware of John's eyes on her as she paid for her purchases.

"Need some help with these, miss?" a bag boy asked.

"No, thanks. I'll just take them myself." Meg pushed her cart full of groceries toward the exit, and John, with his bags in his hands, followed her.

"Have time to stop in for coffee this evening?" he asked.

"I–I'd better not. I—uh—have to get these groceries put away, and I have some things I need to catch up on," she answered evasively. She tried to control the tremor in her voice. It scared her to think how important John Austin was becoming to her. He would soon be gone, and being with him now could only make matters more complicated for her.

Her cool reply registered with Austin, reaffirming his conclusion that she was rooted in a relationship beyond his reach. No matter how strong his attraction to her, he did not choose to put her in the embarrassing position of having to drum up excuses to refuse his offers. "I understand," he told her. "I'll be off, then." He nodded to her and went in search of his car.

When he had turned his back to her, Meg watched him walk across the pavement with his head held high. His muscular arms carried the heavy bags of groceries as though they were filled with feathers. Meg's pulse raced through her veins like a riptide as she allowed her eyes to follow him.

John Austin, you are just the kind of man I hope God will choose for me someday, but I sure wish He would hurry things up a bit! That Ramona is one lucky girl!

Chapter 17

Austin Bruce pulled the final pages of his manuscript from the printer and stacked them neatly in a sturdy corrugated box. Ramona would be pleased to receive the completed book almost a month before the date he had promised it. Her frequent calls were beginning to border on harassment, and he would be glad to put an end to them. Were all literary agents so persistent?

He could get the box in the mail this afternoon, and Ramona would have it, in New York, within forty-eight hours. Unless she had major changes to suggest, she would have the final draft in the hands of his publishers by the end of the month.

Just two months ago, he remembered now, his novel had come to a complete standstill. His characters seemed to be made of cardboard, and no matter how hard he tried, he could not seem to make them come alive on paper. Writer's block had been a new and frightening experience for him. But when his mind had finally perceived a clean, clear image of his protagonist, he had been able to transfer that image to the pages of his manuscript. He had Meg to thank for that. She had helped him bring life to the character, and after that, the rest was easy.

Austin had agonized for hours on end over this novel, but now that he had brought it to conclusion, he felt invigorated and free, happy that he had chosen writing as his career! But it did have limitations. In creating fictional characters, he could mold and manipulate them to look and act as he chose. Not so in real life.

As far as physical appearances went, he would not change one hair on the head of Meg Donnelly. Her beauty did not stop with her outward loveliness, but rather, it permeated her whole being. She was the kind of woman he had always dreamed of finding in real life, but until this summer, that kind of woman could only be found between the pages of his books. If only he could author the real-life story that would make her his partner for life!

It had taken Austin a long time to learn to trust God to write the chapters of his personal life. But ever since his Christian conversion two years ago, he had learned to walk with God, even when the path was difficult to follow. Was it wrong that he now yearned so desperately to take charge of this script himself?

Meg was not the first woman he had found attractive. He had known many women, some of whom he liked and admired very much. There were times when he had even considered making a permanent commitment to one of them. His biological clock seemed to be ticking at an accelerated rate, and like most men his age, he wanted his life to include love and marriage and a family. He had prayed for God to send him someone he could cherish through all eternity.

But he had always stopped short of making that final commitment because he had never felt sure of his choice—until now. Meg affected him in a way no woman ever had before, and he was quite sure no one else ever could.

Now that his novel was finished, he had no reason to stay in North Carolina for the rest of the summer. If he left next week, Meg would be happy. She could move back into her comfortable home instead of living in the crowded confines of her basement, depriving herself of the comforts she deserved.

But just the thought of leaving her turned him inside out. Once he returned to Florida, he would probably never see her again, and that was an idea he simply couldn't accept.

Meg had made it clear to him that his presence was a thorn in her side, and everything he did seemed to irritate her. Furthermore, she had dropped more than one clue that she was already involved in a relationship with another man. But Austin had never been reticent about fighting for the things he wanted out of life, and he wouldn't leave North Carolina without at least letting Meg know the way he felt about her.

But he couldn't declare himself yet. There were a couple of things he needed to clear up first. Why, she did not even know his real name or what he did for a living! He did not want to start their relationship with even a shred of secrecy or deceit between them. Until now, he had always evaded her questions about his personal life, but if he expected to have any kind of chance with Meg, he must open up his life to her and lay everything out on the table. There was no longer a need to avoid recognition anyway, now that his work was complete.

Meg was so completely immersed in her job and with the bookmobile project that she hardly had time for outside activities during the week. He wanted to talk to her at a time and place when he could capture her undivided attention for a few hours. If he could entice her to go away with him on Saturday, he knew just the spot where he would take her. A quiet, romantic setting where he would open his entire life to her like the pages of a book. He would tell her how much he had grown to love her, and unless she sent him packing, he would ask her to be his wife.

In all probability, she would refuse his proposal, but a small shred of hope continued to hammer in his head. If he left North Carolina without declaring his love, he would always wonder what might have been.

Once he had made this decision, Austin felt exhilarated, as though a big burden had been lifted from his shoulders. He had made a plan of action, and even though he did not dare to be optimistic about its outcome, at least he was going to give it his best shot.

Was Meg the woman God had chosen for him, or was God merely tormenting him by dangling an impossible dream before his eyes? If Meg Donnelly was truly the woman God intended for him, then why was she putting up such a strong wall of resistance? But if God planned for the two of them to be joined together, He would show Austin a way to bring Meg into his life, and with God, all things were possible.

Meg left work on Wednesday afternoon an hour past closing time. At five o'clock, Mr. Hanson had asked her to type a sales contract for him, which he wanted to deliver to the seller that night. Meg had never considered herself a typist, but this afternoon there was no one else available for the job.

She pulled up the file on her computer and went to work, filling in all the blanks from the draft copy Mr. Hanson had left on her desk. She finished at six o'clock and took it to him in his office.

"Thank you, Miss Donnelly. I'm sorry you had to work late tonight, but this is very important to the firm. Our buyer is from out of state, and time is of the essence."

"I'm glad I could help," she said. "If there's nothing else then, I'll see you tomorrow."

Meg backed her car from its diagonal space and turned to enter Main Street, but the parking lot exit was blocked by a big, blue truck parked horizontally across the drive. Expecting the truck to move forward into traffic, she waited patiently for a few moments until she realized that the driver was purposely stalling, staring at her with a wide, ugly leer spread across his face. And that evil-looking face was one she clearly recognized. *Bud McLendon!*

Meg's head spun like a runaway top. She choked on great gulps of air as cold, raw fear gripped her like a metal vise.

As soon as Bud was sure that he had her attention, he moved ahead slowly and disappeared from her view, but the image of his malevolent face remained indelibly imprinted on her mind. Meg's hands trembled so violently that she could hardly grasp the steering wheel, and her whole body felt as though she had been doused with ice water. She was in no condition to drive, yet she couldn't just sit there. She considered returning to the real estate office to phone the sheriff and file a complaint. But what could she report? That a man stalled his truck and looked at her? Nothing in Bud McLendon's actions had been illegal, yet his unspoken threat was as real as if he had shouted aloud the same vicious message he had printed on the brick thrown through her kitchen window. His look said it all: *I don't get mad; I just get even.*

Meg forced her eyes to warily peruse the main street in both directions. With no sign of a blue truck anywhere in sight, she began to breathe easier. She saw that Mr. Hanson was locking the front door of the office, and she thought of detaining him long enough to pull herself together before starting the long drive home. He was looking at her with a quizzical expression. How could she describe to him what had just happened?

In the end, she eased her car into the street and turned it toward the road to Mountain View. In her hurry to get home, she broke every speed limit and almost wished for a police officer to come along and stop her.

All the way home, her eyes darted furtively from the highway to her rearview mirror and back again, half expecting to see a blue truck zooming up behind her. She passed several cars, but absolutely nothing on wheels was catching up to her from the rear.

At last, she turned off the highway onto the familiar unpaved road that led toward home. She heaved a sigh of relief as her pent-up emotions slipped out of her like air from a punctured tire.

When she reached her house, she parked her car on the narrow edge of the precipice and sat motionless with closed eyes. *Thank You, God, for bringing me safely home!*

She was afraid that her knees would fold beneath her before she reached her apartment, but her guardian angel must have been riding on her shoulder, because she made it to the door without incident, let herself in with her key, and collapsed on the couch.

The comforting aroma of pot roast and vegetables floated on the evening air. Her dinner in the slow-cooker was ready and waiting, reminding her that she had not eaten since her soup and salad lunch at noon. Suddenly she was ravenous. She thought it strange that she could even think of food after all that had happened today, but perhaps a good meal was exactly what she needed.

She pulled herself from the couch and filled a glass with milk from the refrigerator. She heaped a plate with the tempting one-dish meal from her slow-cooker and sat down alone at the tiny dinette table.

After she had given thanks, she speared a piece of fork-tender meat and raised it to her lips. She was so glad that she did not have to prepare a meal tonight. The strain of the day had completely wiped her out.

The apartment was bathed in silence and made her think of a cave dwelling. She strained to hear the sound of John's printer from upstairs, but all she could hear was the song of night frogs and a distant owl. Although the succulent beef was one of her favorite foods, tonight it seemed rather tasteless, and her vegetables needed seasoning. Restless energy and exhaustion seemed to be at war within her. This night of all nights, she needed someone to talk to.

She rose from the table, her meal only half eaten, and raised her windows, hoping to encourage the evening breeze to sweep away the oppressive heat of the day. She used a small fan to circulate the air, hoping she could cool her rooms before she went to bed. She certainly couldn't go to sleep with the windows unlocked tonight. In fact, she was not certain she could sleep tonight in any case.

It was foolish for her to be so jumpy over that one small incident. Just because Bud McLendon had *looked* at her was no reason for her to become completely unhinged. Why couldn't she put the whole thing out of her mind?

She picked up the phone to call Sandy. Just a few minutes of idle chitchat with a good friend would get her mind back on track. She punched the digits into the phone and waited, but there was no answer. She would try again later, after she had washed her supper dishes.

Meg looked at the six-pound roast staring at her from its resting place on the table. For some reason, she thought of John and the stack of TV dinners he had carted from the grocery store yesterday. Would he think her too forward if she fixed him a plate and took it upstairs to him? Reheated pot roast would surely beat a TV dinner.

Meg considered the idea while she stacked her supper dishes. She was about to scrape her plate into the garbage can when she thought of Harry, that lazy old cat who insisted on making Meg's welcome mat his permanent headquarters.

Although she had not changed her mind about keeping a pet on the premises, John was right in saying that they could not allow the poor animal to starve to death. Feeding Harry would only encourage him to stay, and eventually something would have to be done about him. Perhaps John would agree to take him into Shady Valley to the animal shelter if his owner did not come to claim him soon. Making that decision eased her conscience so that she scraped the remains of her dinner onto a piece of aluminum foil and folded it into a neat little package for Harry.

Meg tried Sandy's number again, but still she received no answer. She didn't even have a good book to read tonight. She thought of John Austin upstairs, dining alone on a TV dinner, and decided that offering to share her supper with him could only be interpreted as a neighborly gesture.

Meg cut thick, generous slices of roast beef and put them on a plate. She surrounded the meat with vegetables and drizzled *au jus* gravy over all. She pulled a roll of plastic wrap from the shelf and stretched it to cover the plate. A meal that had looked unappetizing when she prepared an identical one to eat herself suddenly took on new appeal. She had to admit that it looked pretty tasty.

She combed her hair, picked up the plate, along with the foil containing her supper scraps for Harry, and scuttled up the side of the hill before she had time to change her mind.

Harry was not sleeping in his usual place on the mat. In fact, he was nowhere to be seen. Perhaps he had returned to his owner, and at least one of her problems was solved already. In case the cat returned, she emptied the packet of leftover food into Harry's dish before she knocked on the back door. She stood with her plate in her hands, waiting for John to answer.

He opened the door a thin sliver at first, but when he saw her standing there, he threw it wide. "Meg! What a nice surprise. I was just thinking of you!"

She stepped into the kitchen. "You were?" She was encouraged by the look of pleasure that shone in his warm, dark eyes, a look that seemed to convey a thousand wonderful words. "I was wondering—that is, I was just having my supper and, well, there seemed to be so much for one person, I just wondered if—"

"If you're inviting me for supper, I accept!"

She hadn't prepared herself for such a spontaneous assent. "Well, actually, it's not exactly an invitation. It's more like a sharing of my leftovers." She extended the plate of food, and he took it from her. "I suppose you've already had your supper," she continued, "but this will keep nicely in your refrigerator until tomorrow." She could feel the color rising to her cheeks and used a rush of words to cover her embarrassment. "It's nothing special, really. Just plain old pot roast and vegetables. They've been simmering in my slow-cooker all day."

"I know! That tantalizing aroma has been haunting me all day. I almost hinted for an invitation to join you tonight."

"Oh! Well, actually, I'm not in a position to entertain. My—er—apartment is so small, and I don't have the necessary refinements to invite guests." There was a moment of awkward hesitation as they stood facing each other under the fluorescent kitchen lights across the stone-patterned linoleum. Meg thought of the solitude waiting for her downstairs, and wanting to prolong her stay, she ventured, "I put out some table scraps for Harry, but I didn't see him around anywhere."

"He prowls at night, but I'll be surprised if he doesn't return before morning, and I'm sure he'll appreciate your thoughtfulness. He turns up his nose at the dry cat food I've been buying, but I'm afraid I don't have many tasty scraps to offer him."

Meg started to offer her suggestion about the animal shelter, but something inside her refused to let the words come out. Poor old Harry! What could a few more days hurt? Instead, she said, "Well, I'll be running along, then." Moving slowly, she edged toward the back door, willing him to stop her.

"Wait, Meg. Don't go yet. Stay and I'll make a pot of coffee."

She tried not to appear eager when she accepted his offer. "You might be able to persuade me, if you promise that same gourmet blend you made last time."

Meg watched him scurry around the kitchen, making coffee and placing mugs and napkins on a tray. It felt strange to stand around in her own home acting like a guest, yet she didn't feel free to plunder the cabinets to help him set things up.

"Shall we sit here at the table?" she asked him.

"I like it better outside," he replied, leading the way to the deck.

He put the tray on the glass-topped wicker table and led her to the old oak swing that hung from the roof by thick, brass chains. He handed her one of the mugs and took the other one for himself. The only brightness came from a soft glow of filigreed moon lace formed by leaves and light. They sat side by side, gently swaying as they sipped hot coffee and talked late into the night.

Meg had not planned to tell John about her most recent encounter with Bud McLendon, but sitting on the deck in the cool evening air, she found him so very easy to talk to.

When she had finished the story, he said, "That's not a matter to be taken lightly, Meg." John covered her small hand with his larger one, and a surge of warmth enveloped Meg like a comfortable quilt on a cold winter night. She did not pull her hand from his.

"He didn't actually do anything," Meg said. "I was hesitant to even mention it, lest you might think I'm becoming paranoid."

"No one in his right mind would think that! There's no way to tell what a man like Bud McLendon is apt to do, and you can't be too careful, darling." The word seemed to slip unbidden from his lips, and he hurried his speech to cover it. "One of these days that man is going to push his luck too far and get himself put away where he belongs, but until he does, you need to avoid him like a vine of poison ivy."

Meg hung on to his word of endearment and hardly heard the rest of his comments. *But many people use terms like that in everyday situations,* she reasoned, *even with people they hardly know.* She mustn't allow herself to attach too much importance to such a casual utterance.

"John, I really must be going. It's getting late."

"Meg, I know you're very busy getting ready for the bookmobile dedication, but do you think you could give me a whole day of your time on Saturday? I know where there's a beautiful state park with a spectacular waterfall. We could take a picnic lunch and spend the whole day."

"Why, I don't believe I have any other obligations this Saturday. Yes, I think that would be lovely!" Meg's heart leaped with joyful anticipation, but again she cautioned herself lest she read too much into his invitation. After all, he was still in almost daily communication with Ramona. He would soon be leaving North Carolina, so it was only natural that he would want to visit one of the state's most popular natural attractions.

"I have some things I'm saving to tell you, Meg. Important things that need your undivided attention. I hope you'll hear me out."

"I–I'll look forward to it, John. Until Saturday, then." She started toward the porch stairs, but he grasped her arm and pulled her back.

"Come through the house and go down the back way. It's easier."

He followed her through the living room and kitchen, out to the back porch. "I'll stand here until I hear you lock your door."

"That isn't necessary, John, but—" She hesitated. It was comforting to have someone so concerned about her safety and welfare. "But I would surely appreciate it."

When she turned to smile into his face, their gazes met and locked and refused to let go. Then slowly, he lowered his mouth to hers, and she rose on tiptoe to meet his kiss. When his arms encircled her waist and pulled her close, she slipped her hands to his shoulders and felt herself swirling into an ebb tide, drowned in a sea of ecstasy.

As if waking from a dream, Meg reluctantly pulled out of his arms and pushed herself away from him. "Good night, John."

"Good night, darling."

Chapter 18

How do you want me to handle the children's books, Meg?" Alice Robards was elbow-deep in a box of musty volumes, sorting through them and separating them into various stacks. "Should I try to arrange them according to age, or would you rather have them by subject?"

Meg looked up from her card file and pushed an elusive lock of brown hair from her eyes. She raked the back of her hand across her forehead to wipe away the moisture. In spite of air-conditioning, the library seemed stuffy tonight. "Why don't you just bunch all the juvenile literature together until we get it carded? It's more important to go ahead and get these boxes unpacked to see what we have. We can arrange everything in proper order later."

"You look tired, Meg," Alice said, scowling as she scrutinized her friend's expression. "Why don't we all quit and call it a night?"

"I am a little tired," Meg admitted. "Probably nothing a quick cup of coffee wouldn't cure."

"I was able to squeeze in a short nap after lunch," Alice confessed. "But you've put in a full day at the office, and now this! Go ahead and leave, Meg. The rest of us can finish unpacking the few boxes we have left. We still have tomorrow and all next week to finish everything."

"Aren't we meeting to work Saturday morning?" Cameron Brown asked. "I'm free if you need me."

Meg felt as if she were choking on an apple. "I–I'm afraid I've already committed to something else on Saturday."

"Not to worry," Cameron assured her. "You've already contributed twice as many hours to this project as the rest of us. Those of us who show up on Saturday will do what we can and save the rest for later. Alice is right, Meg. You do look like you need to quit now and go home."

"Well, thanks a lot for the compliments, you guys!" Meg quipped with a good-natured chuckle. "You sure know how to deflate a gal's ego!" But in truth, she was tired to the bone. A warm shower and a glass of milk would make even her lumpy sofa bed seem inviting. "If you're sure. . ."

"We're sure," Alice confirmed. "But I'm going to walk out to the parking lot with you, just to make certain your car hasn't been vandalized again."

"Come walk out with me if you'd like. The break will probably be good for you, but I'm not worried about my car tonight. I told Deputy Scarsdale about our workshop here tonight, and he's having this whole area patrolled until midnight." Meg cleaned her work off the library table and picked up her purse. "I'll be back to help on Monday night. At the rate things are moving along, by next Wednesday we should actually be ready to stack the books onto the shelves of the bookmobile."

On her way toward the exit, Meg stopped to admire some of the books that had been sorted and placed in colored baskets pushed against the wall. "People have been so generous in their donations. Look at these, Alice! They look almost new, as though they've never been read." She picked up a volume and flipped through the crisp pages.

"Actually, that's one of my donations you're holding in your hand. Have you read it, Meg?"

Meg looked at the cover and read the title. "*Dead Men Don't Tell,* by Austin Bruce. No, I don't think that I have. But to be perfectly honest, I'm not into murder mysteries, Alice."

"That book is not as gruesome as its title suggests. In fact, I found it rather refreshing to read a best-seller that wasn't filled with profanity and explicit sex. I'm going to look for more books by that author. Why don't you take it home with you tonight and read it? We don't need it yet, and I think you'll like it."

"I don't seem to find much time to read lately, but thanks. I will take it along and try to read it when I can. I'll get it back here before we need it for the opening of the bookmobile."

"My goodness, Meg. That's what the bookmobile is all about—getting books into the hands of people who want to read. I can't think of anyone who should be more entitled to it than you. Keep it as long as you'd like."

Meg's car sat waiting beneath the bright lights of the parking lot. The two women circled the vehicle, examining it for any signs of foul play. When she was completely satisfied, Meg slid behind the wheel and waited while she watched Alice return to the building.

While she waited,. she picked up the hardback volume Alice had insisted she take home to read. Even the slick paper jacket looked new. Admittedly, Alice had made the book sound interesting. Meg turned it over to examine the back cover, and gulped a sharp intake of air when she saw the clear black-and-white photograph of the author, with his signature boldly penned across one corner of the book jacket: Austin Bruce!

There must be some mistake. This could not be—and yet she knew that it was—the same man who rented her house under the name of John Austin, who had presented himself to her since the beginning of summer under a false name! The same man who, only last night, had held her in his arms and kissed her in the moonlight. The man with whom she had fallen in love, and who she had dared to hope would love her in return. Yet he had not even given her his real name! What else was he hiding that he had not bothered to tell her? Was there no escape in this world from deception and lies?

Last night, this man's tender words had filled her heart with a joy that stretched beyond her own imagination. She had actually believed that his plans for Saturday were contrived by him as a prelude to a lasting relationship between the two of them. Just when she thought she was beginning to know him so well, she discovered that she did not know him at all.

All her life she had waited for a special man, the person whom God had created to be one flesh with her forever. But God would never condone deceit and lies. She must have misread His directives. She would no more commit herself to a relationship with a man she could not trust than she would form a bond with a common thief. In a way, John was a thief; he had stolen her heart under false pretenses. And now she understood why Ramona always called him *Austin*. She called him that because it was his rightful name!

She was startled by a rapping on her car window. How long had she been sitting here in the parking lot? Tears were streaming down her face, and she made no attempt to check them.

"Miss Donnelly, are you all right?" Deputy Scarsdale's flashlight almost blinded her. "What happened? Is someone giving you trouble again?"

"No–no, I'm okay," she said through the closed glass. "I–it's just a personal problem, deputy. I'm fine." She turned the key in the ignition, anxious to get away, to get someplace where she could be alone to think.

Still unconvinced, the deputy directed the beam of his flashlight across the backseat and underneath the car. At last he seemed satisfied. "If you're sure you don't need any help—"

"I'm sure." She tried to force a smile. "Thanks for checking." Meg eased her car out of the parking lot and headed home. How would she ever face John Austin again?

Thinking back on it later, she could hardly remember driving her car along the highway that night, turning up the road that led to her house. Her face was awash with tears that refused to cease. *Lord, I'm trying to trust Your direction for my life, but You're heaping more on my plate than I can handle.*

She parked on the road and slung the strap of her purse over her shoulder. She looked at the book lying on the seat beside her and picked it up gingerly as though it were smelly garbage. She locked her car and stumbled across the yard.

Oh, Lord, spare me! I'm not ready for this yet! Because there on the porch steps, waiting for her, was none other than Austin Bruce!

Austin had been watching for Meg ever since Sandy had called him half an hour ago. According to Sandy, Deputy Scarsdale had called her to report that Meg seemed extremely upset when she drove away from the library parking lot. The sheriff's deputy was worried about her, and had followed her car to just outside the city limits, but seeing nothing unusual, he turned back to town. Deputy Scarsdale knew that Sandy was Meg's friend and her neighbor, and just as an added precaution, he wanted to make sure that Meg arrived home safely. Sandy promptly relayed the message to the man she knew as John Austin, sensing that he had a vested interest in Meg's welfare.

Relief swept over Austin as he saw her step from her car. He hoped that one day soon he could take her away from here until all the trouble with Bud McLendon was settled. He met her halfway across the yard and, seeing her tear-drenched face, held out sympathetic arms to embrace her. "What is it?"

Meg twisted away from him and broke into a run. "Don't touch me! Don't ever come near me again!" In her haste, she almost slipped on the damp, green moss that clung to the flat, gray stepping-stones. Austin, close behind her, managed to catch her just in time to prevent her careening down the slope on her backside. "Meg, what's wrong?" But when he saw the book she carried in her hands, he suddenly understood her distress. "Meg, I can explain everything. Just hear me out."

Her energy spent, Meg's shoulders sagged in resignation. "There is nothing for you to explain. Believe me, I understand everything."

"No, I don't think that you do."

She gave him a contemptuous look. "I'm an old hand in dealing with lies and deception; my father was good at both. That was one of the first lessons I learned as a child. It ruined my parents' marriage." She tried to move away from him, but his hands on her arms restrained her.

"Listen to me, Meg. Lies and deceit may have destroyed your parents' marriage all those years ago, but now you're letting it destroy you! You've held on to that mistrust and animosity all your life, and it's time to let it go. And give me a break! Was it really such a terrible thing that I used a little fabrication to claim a few months of anonymity in order to finish my next book? How was I to predict that I would fall head-over-heels in love with my landlady?"

"You—*what?*"

"Get real, Meg. How can that admission come as a surprise to you? Don't you know how much you have come to mean to me these past few weeks? I had planned to wait until tomorrow to tell you that, to propose to you in a romantic setting beneath the waterfall. But I do love you, Meg, and I had hoped that you were starting to feel the same way about me."

Meg raised her fingers to her temples. "I–I'm so tired and confused. I need some time alone to think, John. Or should I call you *Austin*?"

He skipped over the sarcasm in her voice. "Either way, it doesn't matter. But for the record, my name is *John Austin Bruce*. The name I 'borrowed' is my own. If my small misrepresentation offended you, I offer my sincere apology. But please, Meg, think about what I've said. I want tomorrow to be a special day for us, one that we'll both remember forever."

Meg refused the offer of his arm as she took careful steps toward her door. Austin stood watching her fumble with the lock and then disappear behind her closed door. Sadly, he climbed up the stones that led back to his porch. Meg just needed some space and time to think things through, he decided. As soon as the sun came up in the morning, he would meet her and try to make everything right between them again.

Meg had her warm shower and her glass of milk, just as she had planned, but that was not enough to sooth her heavy heart this night. She wondered if she would ever feel whole again. This crazy summer rental plan had been a foolish idea from the get-go. For the small amount of financial relief it had brought her, she had paid a steep price.

John—she still could not think of him by another name—had said that he loved her! But he had said a lot of things over the past few weeks. How many of them were true, and how many were pure fiction, like the "name game" he played?

But the thing that disturbed her most was his accusation that she harbored resentment carried over from childhood. That was almost the same thing Sandy had said to her before, but it simply was not true! Or was it? She reached for her Bible and opened it to the third chapter of Philippians. She ran her index finger down the page until she came to the familiar thirteenth and fourteenth verses and read them as though seeing them for the first time: "Forgetting those things which are behind, and reaching forth unto those things which are before, I press toward the mark for the prize of the high calling of God in Christ Jesus."

Was she missing the mark by refusing to let go of past hurts? Had she been so afraid of being hurt again that she had closed her eyes to God's plan for her life? *Lord, help me to see clearly the path You have chosen for me, and I will try to follow it.*

Hours later, as she lay twisting and turning in the dark, she heard a noise outside her window. Probably those pesky raccoons invading her garbage can again or Harry returning from his midnight prowl. Whatever it was, she had no desire to cope with it tonight. She covered her head with her pillow and tried to get some sleep.

She must have slept, but for how long she could not guess. She was jolted from her sleep by a blinding ball of light at her door. Seconds later, a deafening blast shook the entire house, and even before she could pinpoint its source, a wall of fire engulfed the room.

Meg screamed and tugged the blanket from her bed. Enveloping her body in the cover, she groped her way toward the door. But in which direction was her door? She was completely disoriented.

All around her she could hear the hot, angry flames crackling like popcorn. Her whole apartment had turned into a blazing inferno. The last thing that she remembered was the terrible scent of singed hair and burning flesh, and she realized too late that it was her own.

Chapter 19

Meg tried to open her eyes to identify the source of the voices swirling around her head like an eddy. Who were these people in her apartment, and why were they here? She must be having a terrible nightmare. Inky blackness surrounded her. She tried to cry out, but the only sound she could produce was a weak mew.

"Nurse, look! I think she's beginning to wake up!"

Meg recognized Sandy's voice, but she could not force her lips to form the name. What was Sandy doing here in the middle of the night, anyway? And why was there a nurse? She tried to lift her head from the pillow.

"Meg, it's me, Sandy. Everything's going to be okay. Just lie back and try to relax."

"I can't see you!" Meg whispered through swollen lips. "What's happened to me?"

"You can't see because your eyes are bandaged, but the doctor says you're going to be all right. You're in a hospital in Asheville. They airlifted you here on a 'copter last night. Don't you remember any of what happened?"

Meg's head was whirling, but she struggled to bring her thoughts into focus. "A fire! Was there a fire?"

"Yes, that's right. But you mustn't think about any of that now. Just rest and try to regain your strength."

"I have to know, Sandy. Tell me what happened. Why can't I get these bandages taken off so that I can see?" She tried to raise her hands to pull the covering from her eyes, but her arms and hands felt like lead weights.

"You'll have to talk to the nurse about that, Meg. And the doctor thinks it's best to wait until later to talk about what happened. Just try not to worry. I'll stay here with you for as long as you need me."

"Quit treating me like a child, Sandy. I have a right to know what happened, and I want to know now!"

Sandy heaved a sigh of resignation. She knew Meg well enough to be certain that she would not let up until she heard the whole story. Might as well get it over with! "There was an explosion. Someone placed a homemade pipe bomb by your basement door. The good news is that there was a witness. They've arrested Bud McLendon and have him locked up in the county jail. He's not likely to be out for a long, long time."

"John! What about John! Was he hurt?"

"He—he would be here if he could, Meg, but—"

"Never mind that. I don't expect him to come to see me. I just want to make sure he's not hurt."

"Well, he's. . ." She hesitated.

"He is hurt! Oh, Sandy, how bad is it? Where is he?"

"Calm down, Meg. He's going to be all right. He's in a room right down the hall. Meg, he saved your life last night!"

"What do you mean?"

"That explosion rocked the whole house. It literally jolted John out of his bed. He ran outside to see what had happened. He got a good look at the truck and its driver before he sped away, but when John saw the fire gutting your apartment, he bypassed your stepping-stones and jumped down the grade to your door in one giant leap. In spite of a broken ankle, he ran right through the flames and found you huddled on the floor, swaddled in a blanket. He picked you up like a sack of potatoes and carried you to safety just seconds before the whole building collapsed. Oh, Meg, I didn't want to have to tell you about all this until you were stronger, but you insisted. Nurse, you'd better come here. She's trembling like a leaf. I'm afraid the shock was too much for her."

Austin lay between sterile white sheets and uttered a prayer of thanksgiving. Meg was alive! He had come so close to losing her last night. Her hair was singed, but that would grow back. It was her eyes that worried him. The doctors told him that the bandages would be removed next week, and then they would be able to evaluate her sight.

Austin prayed that she would not lose her vision. She had such an immense appreciation for the beauty of God's creation. Today was Saturday, the day they had planned a picnic by the big waterfall. God willing, he would take her there one day soon and tell her all the things he carried in his heart.

He had made a great many mistakes, and he had a lot of explaining to do. He hoped that the doctors would let him sit in a wheelchair later today so that he could visit Meg in her room and start to put things right between them.

Pastor Blake had visited him this morning. Church members had already started a prayer chain for Meg and for him. No wonder the doctors called them both "living miracles"! Meg's burns were only first degree and should heal without disfiguring scars. His own beet-red face stung like a bad case of sunburn, but his only serious burns were the ones on his forearms, the same arms that had miraculously allowed him to carry Meg from the blazing inferno. As soon as his broken ankle mended so that the cast could be removed, he would be as good as new.

Meg's eyes were his greatest concern, as well as the shock that she suffered. She was in for another great shock when she learned that the home she loved so much had been completely devoured by fire. Every piece of furniture and every dish and doily, gone forever! Few people realized how much those things meant to Meg, but Austin knew. How would she react to such a loss?

A knock drew his eyes to the open door. "Oh, Sandy. Come in. How is she?"

"How are you? That's what I came to find out."

"I'm fine. The doctor says I may be able to go home tomorrow. But you didn't answer my question. How is Meg?"

"I honestly don't know how to answer you, John. She forced me to tell her what happened, and since she heard the whole story, she's hardly spoken a word. It's like she's entered a different world. We've been best friends for a long time now, and I've never known her to be like this before. I feel responsible, but she just wouldn't let up until she heard everything."

"I'm going to request a wheelchair after lunch so that I can go in to see her."

"I–I'm not sure that's wise at this time."

"Has she said she didn't want to see me?"

"Not in so many words, but. . ."

"I won't go if you feel my presence would upset her," he said. "But please tell her I want to talk to her. She doesn't have to say anything; just listen to what I have to say."

"I'll ask her," Sandy said, "but please be patient with her. This whole thing is going to take a lot of time."

"Did someone call in the order to the florist as I requested?"

"I believe one of the Pink Ladies took care of the arrangements. I saw the flowers when they were delivered, and they are beautiful! But of course you know that Meg can't see them yet. Perhaps if things go well—"

"She'll be able to see the ones I'll send her next week," Austin said with a firm air of confidence. "Until then, she'll just have to be content to smell them."

"Where will you go when they let you leave, John? Back to Florida?"

"Yes, I'll have to. I have no other place to go, and not even any clothes to wear. Do you suppose Jim would mind shopping for me, just to get me something to go home in?"

"He's planning on stopping in to see you this afternoon. Just tell him what you need, and he'll be glad to help." After a few thoughtful moments, Sandy asked, "Once you leave, will we ever see you again?"

"But of course! I want to be with Meg when the doctors take the bandages off her eyes. I wanted to tell her that myself, but if she isn't ready to let me see her, then just tell her what I said. Whether she wants me or not, I will be back to see her next week."

Chapter 20

For seven long days, Sandy kept her bedside vigil. A chain of women from the church offered to set up a schedule to help by taking turns beside Meg's bed, but except for a few hours each night, Sandy maintained her post.

Although Meg rarely spoke, Sandy continued to ply her with words of assurance, spending endless hours reading passages of scripture from the Gideon Bible she found in the drawer of the bedside table. Sometimes she read chapters she knew were Meg's favorites, like the Twenty-third Psalm, but most often she read from a list of suggestions John Austin had left with her. She wasn't sure what criteria he had used to make his choices. Were these verses that Meg had told him were her favorites, or were they pieces of scripture that John felt she needed at this particular time? Although Sandy did not understand some of his selections, she faithfully followed his suggestions.

From Philippians, she read, "Forgetting those things which are behind, and reaching forth unto those things which are before, I press toward the mark for the prize of the high calling of God in Christ Jesus." And from the fourth chapter of Ephesians, "Let all bitterness, and wrath, and anger. . .be put away from you, with all malice."

On Saturday morning, Sandy leaned over the rail of Meg's bed and reminded her, "Today is the day the bandages are coming off of your eyes, and, God willing, you will be able to see again!" Sandy herself was excited, and she hoped that this news would ignite at least a small spark of interest, but Meg's face remained expressionless, just as it had for the past seven days.

Sandy had heard nothing from John Austin. Had he forgotten his promise to return? Or perhaps he had simply been physically unable to travel so soon after suffering his injuries in the fire.

Last week, when John had been released from the hospital, Sandy had delivered his message and was surprised that Meg had seemed less than delighted. Before the fire, Sandy had begun to think that she detected sparks of romance igniting between those two. John certainly exhibited all the classic signs of a man in love, but she must have misread

Meg completely. Meg had made it very clear that she did not want to see or hear from him.

Sandy picked up the Bible and in her soft, melodic voice, began again to read aloud. Scripture reading seemed to be the only thing that brought a look of peace to Meg's face.

Flight Number 2658 landed on schedule at the Asheville International Airport, and first-class passengers were allowed to disembark.

Austin had become adept at using his crutches and was the first passenger off the plane. He went straight to the telephone and made his daily call to the hospital. After the nurse on the third floor assured him of Meg's continued improvement, his next stop was the car rental agency where he arranged to rent a car for the next few days. Thankfully, the injury to his left foot was not an impediment to his driving ability.

He hobbled over to the turntable to claim his baggage, a brand-new suitcase filled with brand-new clothes, and caught the shuttle to find and claim his car.

He was as nervous as a bridegroom. How would Meg react to his presence now that she had had a week to think things through? Her bandages were due for removal at two o'clock this afternoon. He prayed that she would allow him to be there beside her, holding her hand when she first looked out at the world. No matter what the outcome, he wanted her to know that he would love her and support her for all the years ahead. With a new beginning, they could face any future as long as they were together.

Meg walked in a valley, deep in the cool, gray shadows that separated life from death, but she did not walk alone. Christ was beside her, leading her in the paths of righteousness.

She had been wrong about so many things, but none of them mattered anymore. When she first learned that her house had been destroyed, part of her felt destroyed too, and she was certain she would never be whole again.

Strangely, with her eyes swathed in bandages, she was now able to see things more clearly than she had ever seen them before. She had been like the foolish man whose house was built on sand, and the winds had come and blown it away. Nothing had been as important to her as that house on the mountain, and all the things that it contained. She had once believed that her grandmother's memory, along with the legacy of her wisdom and love, were somehow tied up in that house. But now she knew that this was not true.

Of course she had loved that house and all that it meant to her, but the house was gone now, and nothing could change that. What mattered now was the remnant that was left for her. Her real treasures were laid up in heaven where neither moth nor rust could corrupt, nor thieves break through and steal—and where not even fire could consume—and her faith in God would be strengthened through this adversity.

"Miss Donnelly? Are you awake?" Meg recognized her doctor's voice and nodded her head. "I am going to remove the bandage from your eyes as soon as Dr. Hadley comes to assist me. Are you excited about that?"

Meg was not sure how she should answer him. Yes, she would be happy to be free of the clumsy gauze bindings, but excited? No, a better word would be prepared. She had turned everything over to God, and she was prepared now to accept His plan for her life.

"Meg?" Another voice! This one she recognized, too. John—or Austin—what did a name matter? He had saved her life, and now he had returned to be here beside her. For the first time in a week, she smiled.

He reached for her hands and smothered them in his own. The steady pressure of his fingers flowed through her like a comforting glass of warm milk. Other hands were propping her upright and slowly unwinding the gauze from around her head. When she felt the last piece of cotton fall from her face, she dared to open her eyes.

The first thing that she saw was the velvet brown of his eyes gazing into hers. "John! I can see you! You came back to me!"

Doctors hovered over her, asking questions and shining their pencil-thin flashlights into her eyes, but at last they left the room, and only John remained.

"Meg," he began, "I never meant to deceive you. I wanted you to know everything about me. That's why I planned the day at the waterfall. If you'll just let me explain—"

"Not now, John. There will be plenty of time for that later. I have some explaining of my own to do, but for now, it's enough just to know that you came back."

"How could I not? The doctors say that you can leave the hospital tomorrow, and Sandy has fixed up Beth's room for you. She wants you to stay at her house until you decide on something permanent. I've rented a car, so I can come for you in the morning and help you get settled."

"John, I want to go back to the house first. My house." The startled look on his face made her realize that he misunderstood, and she hastened to explain. "Don't worry, John. I know the house is gone. I've come to terms with that. But I can't put it to rest until I've gone back to see the spot where it stood."

"Meg, I'm not sure that's a wise—"

"Please, John. Trust me. I know what I'm doing."

They stood together, hand in hand, looking at the charred ruins that were once a home. Tears rolled down Meg's cheeks as she said good-bye to the house she had grown to love.

"Are you all right?" John put his arm around her and pulled her close to him.

"Yes, I'm fine. This is rather like the sadness we experience when we attend the burial of a dear friend." She used the back of her hand to wipe moisture from her face. Suddenly, another distressing thought occurred to her. "Oh, John, what do you suppose happened to poor old Harry? I can't bear to think that he was burned in the fire!"

Meg could not understand why John's face broke into a wide grin. "Well," he said, "there's good news and bad news."

"What is it? Tell me. Is Harry still alive?"

"Well, yes and no."

His teasing was maddening, but she was sure that he would not joke about it if the story had a tragic ending. "John Austin, wipe that silly grin off your face and tell me what's going on."

"Harry, well, he—she—it seems like I'm not the only one around here who's been playing 'the name game.' I think our friend, Harry, is really *Harriet*. And Harriet has deserted us and moved her squatter's claim to a spot beneath Sandy's back steps. She's taken up residence and produced a fine litter of baby kittens. So now you'll have to pick out four new names. I kind of favor Tom, Dick, and Harry, and then there's the runt of the litter, Jane Doe."

Meg laughed for the first time in over a week. "Surely a fiction writer of your talents can come up with something more original than that!"

"Well, let's just go look at them and see what you think." Austin led her back to the car, and with one backward glance, she slid into the passenger seat.

Ironically, Meg thought, *now there's plenty of room here to park a dozen cars!*

Epilogue

I'm afraid we're going to run out of punch," Cameron complained to Alice. "I never dreamed this many people would show up for the dedication of our bookmobile, especially after it had been postponed for two weeks."

"I'll send Sid to the store to pick up some more bottles of ginger ale, and we'll just mix that in. No one is going to care, as long as it's cool and wet. Look at the way they're lined up to shake hands with Meg and Austin."

"Well, no wonder! We've never had a real celebrity author signing books in our library before. Just think, he's been right here in our midst all summer, and we didn't even know it! And Meg's sort of like a celebrity herself."

"She is, isn't she? When you think about it, there probably wouldn't even be a bookmobile if Meg hadn't started it."

"And with Austin Bruce donating the proceeds from all those books he's signing, I'd say we'll have our shelves full without ever having to hold another garage sale."

"Come on. Let's sneak away from the refreshment table and go over to see them. We've served most of the guests already, and the rest can just help themselves."

"What about the ginger ale for the punch?"

"Oh, forget the punch. There's a water cooler over there if anyone is that thirsty."

Meg sat at the table next to Austin, selling books and passing them over to him for his autograph. Happiness spilled out of her eyes. She had already sold two boxes of books, and the crowds kept coming. Austin's hand must surely be cramping by now!

"Miss Donnelly?"

Meg looked up into a face that was at once familiar and yet completely transformed into someone she had never seen before. "Billy McLendon! How wonderful that you could come!"

The child's eyes had lost their haunted look, she noted, and now sparkled like clear, green glass marbles. His skin was smooth and tanned, with neither bruise not blemish, and his once pitifully thin frame had metamorphosed into that of a sturdy, healthy boy.

"You've—you've grown taller, Billy."

"Yes'm. My mom—my new mom—she says she can't hardly keep me in britches, I'm growin' so fast." Then he dropped his gaze and stared at the floor. "I reckon you hate my daddy. I'm sorry for what he done."

Meg hastened to assure him, "No, of course I don't hate your father. There's been far too much hate already. In fact, I'm praying for him, hoping he will get help for his problems, and I'm praying for you, too, Billy."

At her encouraging words, the child raised his eyes again and looked directly into her face. "I sure am happy about the new bookmobile, even if I won't be around here to use it. It sure is mighty nice."

Meg was pleased to hear confidence and pride resonating in his voice. "Where will you be attending school next year, Billy?"

A pleasant-looking woman standing behind Billy answered for him. "We're moving upstate as soon as the adoption is finalized." She extended her hand toward Meg. "I'm Helen Grayson. Billy has talked so much about you, Miss Donnelly. He wanted very much to come today."

"I'm so glad that you both were able to make it!" After shaking Helen's hand, Meg reached beneath the table and pulled a book from the box she had packed especially for the children who came to the opening. "Here, Billy, you take this book and stand in that line, so Mr. Bruce can sign it for you. It's not one of his stories, but you can still collect his autograph."

"Thanks, Miss Donnelly. I've still got that book you gave me at school, and I reckon I've read it about a million times already."

Helen waited until Billy was out of hearing range before she said, "He's coming along just fine now, Miss Donnelly, although he had some rough adjustments at first. Billy doesn't know the details of all those terrible things Bud did, but he knows his dad's in jail for breaking the law. We've explained to him that prison may be able to provide help for his father's drinking problems. Billy loves his dad, but from the beginning, he has been adamant about not wanting to return to his father's house, and I think he feels secure with us. My husband and I consider ourselves truly blessed to have a son like Billy. We've always wanted a child, but. . ." Her voice trailed off, quavering.

"I'd say Billy is receiving his share of blessings too, Helen. He's a fine boy, and he deserves a new start."

Pastor Blake and his wife worked their way up to the table. "This must be a very exciting day for you, Meg."

"More than exciting, Pastor. God is really pouring out His blessings on us today."

"They're there every day, but sometimes we just aren't able to recognize them."

ෙ

When the last book had been signed and the punch bowl drained dry, Austin led Meg to his car and opened the door for her. He circled the car and slid in beside her. "I think you'd have to say that the dedication of the new bookmobile was a huge success, thanks to you, Miss Donnelly. But now I think I'd better take you home. I had strict orders from Sandy to have you back in the house by suppertime. She doesn't want you to overdo it until you've had time to regain your strength."

"She's like a mother hen," Meg said, smiling.

As Austin's car sped along the familiar highway, Meg leaned her head against the back of the seat and marveled at the surrounding scenery. The sun was dropping fast in the western sky, outlining the mountaintops with orange brilliance. She had never fully appreciated her eyesight until she was threatened with losing it. As she drank in the picturesque view, she could almost hear the psalmist singing, "I will lift up mine eyes unto the hills, from whence cometh my help. My help cometh from the Lord, which made heaven and earth."

As the powerful car ground its way up the hill, Meg was surprised to see that Austin drove right past Sandy's house without slowing. Half a mile up the mountain, he pulled into what used to be Meg's driveway and killed the engine.

"Meg, your house may be gone, but this beautiful site still belongs to you. I know it can never be the same for you, but someday you should have another home here on this very spot, with a big redwood deck across the front, where you can listen to the brook running by your door."

"I know, I've been giving that some thought."

After a few moments of silence, Austin spoke in a soft murmur. "Have you been giving any thought to me, and the things I told you? Because I do love you, Meg, with all my heart, and I guess I always will. I'd like to help you build that house, bigger this time, with room for a family and maybe even a cat!"

"John Austin Bruce, are you proposing to me?" She tilted her smile up to his face, and the invitation was too good for him to resist. He gathered her in his arms and kissed her lips, and when she joyfully responded, the intensity of his kiss grew from that of a gentle breeze to a full-blown tornado. The two of them were caught in its swirl, spiraling as helplessly as Dorothy and Toto, until at last she pushed herself away from him and drew a deep breath.

"Was that a yes?" he asked.

"Yes, but only if you promise to let me choose the cat. Oh, John—Austin—whatever! In spite of your crazy name game, I do love you so!" She pulled his face down to hers and claimed another kiss.

"While we're playing 'the name game,'" he said, "I'd like to make a suggestion about changing your name. What would you think about changing *your* name to mine?"

"Meg Bruce! It has a nice ring. I think I'm going to like that." He kissed her again, and when she came up for air, she remembered something else. "Just one more question before we leave 'the name game.'-"

"Yes? What is it? Ask me anything, my darling!"

"John, who is Ramona?"

Flip over for another great novel!

CONDO MANIA